Death in a Northern Town 2

No Rest for the Living

By Peter Mckeirnon

ISBN-10: 1500244643

ISBN-13: 9781500244644

The work in this book is fiction. Although place names may be real, characters and events are a product of the author's imagination. Any resemblance to actual events and characters are entirely coincidental. The reproduction of this work in full or part is forbidden without written consent from the author.

Copyright @ 2014

Join the infected – Facebook / Death in a Northern Town

Cover designed by Wise Owl Imagery – Ian Hewitt

Pre-chapter images by Paul Leech

Undeadications Page image by Kyle Doyle

Proof read by Kathryn Begley

Proof read and edited by Anna Anderson

Undeadications Page

Laura McVey, Vikki Ridgway, Aaron Spencer, Mary Walton, Jo Berry, Kelly Jones, Niky Perrow, PJ Horton, Kerrie Ross, Matt Livesey, The Bignalls, Paul Azrael Phoenix, Mandi Varrie, George A Romero, Lucy Heatley, Jessie Heatley, Andyy Fisher, Vicky Beech, Ceris Breckell, Julie Mercer, Sam Morgan, Cegsy Boo Breckell, John Breckell, Julie James, Donna Worthington, Michael Towns, Keilan – John Worthington, Erin – Elise Chukuma, Simon "killed in episode one" Martindale, Amber Lane, Sharon Ludgate, Wesley Jones, Kim Coakley, Shaun Nield, Tony Greenhalgh, Jess Smith, Phil Axford, Patsy Ward, Renata Davies, Hannah Gest, Neil Thornton, Karina Carr, Vicky Hannigan, John McGrath, Dave Dineley, Diane Moore, Phil Moss, Sean Kelly, Phil Humphreys, Caroline Ouseley, Clare Sing, Scott Edwards, Glyn Owen, Melanie Baker – Owen, Lisa Downing, Kearon Allford, Gimps, Ben Wain, Vic Smith, Nykie Brady, Peter Beck, Gary Walker, Susan Evans, Darren Gibbons, Craig "Scabby" Tessyman, Keith Ross, Jenna Moore, Thomas John Moore, Sandra Looker, Andrea Jackson, Andy Jackson, Joanne Bradburne, Kev Hughes, Emily Wood, Heather Nicholls, Little Ted, Mike Brownbill, Valerie Shiels, Charlotte Cross, Lisa Edwards, Paul Lunt, Bill Houghton, Gary Whitehead, Courtney Dunbavand, Neil Gallagher, Tobi Burgers, Ian Woods, Claire Woods, Beth Woods, Matthew Woods, Ged Woods, Louise Yasities, Chris Phillips, Laurel 'The Slayer' Martindale, Stephen Fogg, Ian 'Iggy' Lee, Simon 'Simon Dooley' Dooley, Emma Greenhalgh, Mike 'The Slayer' Wharton, Sarah Layton, Simon Hallsworth, Kate Pitcher, Julia Dawn 'of the Dead' Kelly, Jenny Shaw & Andy Hayes, Leo 'Zombie King' Deathe, Quirkles, Paul Hillan, Ian Charles Bratt, Helen 'Dead as a Dodo' Coakley, one Eyed wee Jimmy Russell, Amanda George, Neil Davis, Linda Gallagher, Tanya Leyshon & Dan Evans from Helsby, Tracey Burton, Cathie Ventham & Neil Marston, Rod Burton, Darren & liesa Rowlinson-Cooper, Nymphetamine Nat.

When Death Comes To Town

By

Faster than Bulls

Inspired by Death in a Northern Town

Watch the music video on Youtube

Faster than Bulls – When Death Comes To Town

Download the single available now from iTunes and Amazon MP3

Dedicated to the residents of Runcorn,

Alive, dead and undead alike.

You wouldn't want to be me,

You'd be cursed to be near me,

These streets they will take you,

Leave now they will break you,

There's death here in my town.

There's a sickness in this town,

Where the dead don't die they surround,

Pain is the only sound,

When death comes to your town.

John Diant, survivor

Journal Entry 8

My name is John Diant. Father, brother, head of the anti-mayonnaise society and slayer of the living dead. It's over a day since I last updated this journal. Over a day since my daughter Emily, her boyfriend Jonathon and my retro friend 80s Dave and I made it to my brother Butty's house. After fighting the undead population of Runcorn to get here, we thought we'd be safe... but nothing could have prepared us for what came next.

I'll recount events the best I can but it won't be easy. I think I've had three hours sleep since the zombie apocalypse came to my town. Add to that the two delicious, filling and nutritional tins of spam I've eaten since the outbreak and the result is my mind is not as sharp as it should be. But I've made a promise to myself to keep this journal as up to date as possible. If my brother's right then it will be journals like mine that people turn to when this thing is over. Anne Frank? You've got nothing on me girl. You might have been the hide and seek champion of Nazi occupied Amsterdam but in zombie overrun Runcorn, nowhere is safe.

I've learnt a lot since the recently deceased came back to life and my home town went straight to hell - Not just about zombies but about myself too. For instance, I've learnt that I have the gag reflex of a 14 year old boy who's just drank his first litre bottle of strong cider and I've learnt that I know very little about my teenage daughter.

But hey, what parent does know what their kid really gets up to right? There was me thinking Emily was spending her time dancing around her bedroom and chatting with her friends about boy bands, make-up, and the latest celebrity gossip, when in reality she had a boyfriend and was as prepared for the zombie apocalypse as I was unprepared. But as much of a shock as it was, I'm thankful. I'm thankful for her boyfriend Jonathon because if it wasn't for him and his ability to act first and think later, Emily and I may not be alive right now. OK, so he did accidentally kill a man but that man was about to turn into one of the undead so I can forgive him. He quickly proved an asset to our dysfunctional team and I'm glad Emily had someone like him looking out for her when it mattered most. I'm also thankful that Emily isn't the innocent girl I thought she was. Luckily for me, my survivalist nut job of a brother had a bigger influence on her life than I thought and I'm grateful for that, I truly am. I had spent the majority of yesterday trying my hardest to come to terms with the end of the world and the fact that the very people I shared my town with had turned into flesh hungry monsters. My daughter on the other hand adjusted immediately, having no problem disposing of her once human fellow Runcornians. In fact, it would appear that out of our little band of survivors, the only one of us that had any difficulty coming to terms with the zombie Armageddon was me! Take 80s Dave for example. When not smoking and listening to retro tunes through his original 1980s Sony Walkman, killing zombies came as easy to him as being a crazy bastard does for my brother. Fortunately, the company I'm keeping has started to rub off on me but I still have a long way to go before slaying the living dead becomes anything close to a normal activity.

So then, here goes. When I last updated this journal I was readying myself for some shut eye. After what was the second worst day of my life, sleep was a welcome distraction. Only, I wasn't asleep for as long as I would have liked thanks to my crazy ass sibling.

"Wakey, wakey little brother," Butty whispered.

I opened my eyes to see the grinning and heavily camouflaged face of my brother inches from mine. Not the worst sight I've ever woken up to but it was close.

If you've read my first journal you will know that my brother, being the disturbed survivalist genius that he is, secured his house by firstly boarding up all windows and doors. Then realising that the zombies could sniff out the living, he slayed several of the undead, chopped up their rotting body parts and nailed them to the exterior of the house to mask his meaty fragrance. Oh yes I nearly forgot, he also decapitated five of the bastards and stuck their heads on spikes, displaying them outside his front door. Butty doesn't do subtle.

As an extra security measure he removed the staircase from the ground to first floor so if zombies broke through the boarded up doors and windows, they would have no way of reaching us in our elevated position. That is unless they had somehow mastered the art of Parkour Free Running. If that was to happen then we'd be fucked!

"What do you want Butty?" I asked.

"Come with me, I want to show you something," he replied.

"Last time you said that we were kids and you made me look out of our grandparent's bathroom window into Paula Brownrigg's back garden so I could see her sunbathing topless," I said.

"Oh yeah, I'd forgotten about that! That was some sight wasn't it?" Butty asked, with eyes wide and full of wonder as he recalled his forgotten memory.

"Some sight? Butty she was pushing seventy. I nearly lost my sight altogether!" I replied, rubbing the sleep from my eyes, "I wonder what happened to her? Died years ago I suspect."

"Died recently actually. Her head's on one of the spikes outside the front door. I'm surprised you didn't notice but then again, it wasn't her face you remembered was it," Butty smiled.

"No it wasn't. I can't believe you've stuck her head on a spike," I said, shocked at my brother's revelation.

"Dead is dead little bro. Friends, neighbours, acquaintances... Once they turn into shufflers they're all the same to me. You knew the other four heads too. Ian Hewitt from over the road, Gemma Potter from Clifton Farm and Andy Osborne and Lindsey Axford from school. Do you remember her husband, Phil Axford? Well he was going to be stuck on spike number six but his bonce was in such a mess after I'd finished with it, it hardly resembled a head at all. So I chopped him up and nailed him to the house instead. I decided to stick with just the five spikes after that," Butty said matter of factly.

"Oh man, really? Did you have to use the heads of people we know?" I gagged, swallowing the build-up of saliva in my mouth.

"We live in a small town John. You don't have to travel far to see a familiar face around these parts and in your case, you just have to step out of the front door to see five! Word of advice, if the news about the heads out the front upset you then you best not look in the back garden," Butty advised.

"Why, how many more of my friends have you killed?" I asked, concentrating hard on keeping the contents of my stomach where they belonged.

"Oh not many. Just Kevin Rice, Peter Walker, Ross Ocego, Neil Davis, Paul Lancaster, Jax Mannering, Darren Littler... Actually I broke my hammer killing that dead bastard.

Then there was Charlotte Cross, Claire Brooks, Greg Beesley, Gary Littler, Clare Sing, Matt Livesey, Mel Simo, Kim Bunting, Neil Thornton, Geoff Cross, Caroline Ouseley, Kev Hughes, Lora Short, John Lewis, Emma McGibbon, Debbie Cleary, Dave Dineley, Gary McGuinness and err… Craig Tessyman. I think that's it but there could be more," Butty boasted.

"Jesus Butty, we're one day into the apocalypse and you've killed more people than Spanish Flu! If I didn't know better I'd say you had purposely sought out everyone I knew that was infected, somehow managed to herd them all here and kill them just to piss me off!" I said.

"Don't talk daft John, I've had better things to do than bugger about killing zombies just to annoy my little brother. It's as I said, we live in a small town and when you've lived here as long as we have you get to know people. It's just unfortunate that the majority of people these days have turned into flesh hungry monsters. Look at it this way, by killing almost everyone you know, I've saved you the heart ache of having to see them as zombies. I've actually done you a favour when you think about it," he explained, rationalising his actions as only he could.

"You're all heart Butty, always thinking of others," I replied.

"All in a day's work John, no biggy. Anyway, forget about all that, I need to show you something. Come on let's go," he said.

"Butty it must be about 5am, I'm shattered, full of painkillers and my head is spinning at the news of your killing spree. Can't this wait a little while longer?" I asked.

I had put my back out slipping in zombie head splatter whilst attempting to rescue my daughter a day earlier and, although the pain had dulled enough to allow for fluid movement, I wasn't sure how much was down to the medication we had liberated from a medical centre. To be honest, I was quite happy to carry on pill popping rather than find out.

"Trust me, you'll want to see this, now move your arse and follow me," Butty instructed, making his way to the hallway.

"Well this better be good. If you've woken me up just so you can show me more of your tinned spam collection I'll force feed you the stuff till it comes out of your ears," I said following my brother.

Out on the hallway he lowered the ladder leading to the attic. It had been years since I last ventured up there. He had converted it into an extra room and fitted a skylight long before Emily was born. He said it would add value to his house but what he really wanted it for was to search for aliens.

The attic was just as I remembered it. The large skylight with my brother's telescope looking through and an old fold out wallpaper pasting table used as a desk with radio transmission equipment on top. My brother was part of a local 'club' called Aliens of Runcorn Spotters Elite. Yep, you read that right, A.R.S.E! There were many members of A.R.S.E. and they all communicated using Citizens Band radio transmitters or C.B. radios as they are more commonly known. Obviously, the people of A.R.S.E. had never met face to face. Alien contact is a concept deemed perfectly reasonable with A.R.S.E. members but human contact? Not so much.

"I see you've still got your alien observatory up and running and oh look, more spam!" I said, spying another large collection of tins under the makeshift desk.

"You'll be grateful for all that spam in a few months when food supplies are depleted. Up to five years those tins of delicious salty pork goodness can last. Five years!" Butty exclaimed. "Anyway, I didn't bring you up here to show you the remainder of my spam collection. If I did we'd be down in the cellar where I have another 600 tins. I brought you here to show you this…"

Butty switched on his C.B radio, pressed the 'speak' button and spoke into the microphone.

"This is Lone Wolf come in, over," he said.

"Lone Wolf? Who the hell do you think you are? Chuck Norris or some kind of bad ass? Does whoever it is you're trying to contact know that Lone Wolf runs with a pack now toowooooooo!" I said, doing my very best howling wolf impression.

"Alright smart arse it's just a handle. You've got to have a handle to distinguish yourself from everyone else. It's C.B. rules. You would know that if you'd had joined Alien Spotters of Runcorn Elite when I asked you to," Butty replied.

"It's called A.R.S.E. butty, ARSE!" I said.

"Come in Lone Wolf this is Sky Watcher here. How's it going over there, over?" came the sultry female voice through the speakers of the C.B. radio.

"That's Sky Watcher," my brother said excitedly.

"You don't say?" I replied sarcastically.

"Ten four Sky Watcher this is Lone Wolf, all good here, over good buddy," he said.

"What the fuck was that? You're not Burt Reynolds you know? This isn't Smokey and the Bandit!" I said through a fit of laughter.

"That's how people talk to each other over Citizens Band radio, it's the rules. Have you never watched the film

Convoy?" Butty replied, his camouflaged covered forehead wrinkling in anger at my constant mocking.

"Yes I have but this isn't the Deep South and you're not a trucker. You're a nut job spam fanatic who stuck the heads of his dead friends and neighbours on spikes," I said to the crazy bastard.

"Good to hear you're OK Lone Wolf, I've missed your voice," Sky Watcher replied flirtatiously.

My brother puffed his chest out in hearing her words. He was obviously sweet on this girl and hearing her enticing reply filled him with confidence.

"It's good to hear your voice too Sky Watcher. My brother, my niece and a rag tag band of survivors showed up on my doorstep a few hours back. Lucky they found me when they did. They were in pretty rough shape by all accounts but fortunately for them, Lone Wolf was here to save the day," Butty boasted.

"What the hell are you talking about? Rough shape? We're all fine. Oh I see what's happening here, you've got a crush on this girl haven't you? That's why you're acting the big man. So come on then spill the beans what's she like? Do you know her real name?" I said.

"C.B. rules John. No names, handles only. I only know her as Sky Watcher and that's good enough for me," he replied.

"Give me the receiver I want to speak to her," I said, reaching to take it from his hand.

"No fuck off!" he snapped, slapping my hand away.

"That's just like you Lone Wolf, always putting the needs of others first. You're a hero Wolfman and I hope your brother and his friends appreciate how lucky they are to have such a great guy like you around to help," Sky Watcher swooned, feeding my brothers ever expanding ego.

"Hey Lone Wolf I almost forgot to tell you, there have been no further incidents since the initial attack. It was messy and it wasn't easy with just an old rusty saw but I chopped those deaders up good and stuck their rotting body parts to my house like you told me to and not one zombie has bothered me since," She continued.

A large smile spread across my brother's face and he looked across to me smugly, revelling in his new hero status and who could blame him? He had found a way to hide us from the undead. What I was struggling to get my head around was that he had shared his discovery with others. Of course he was going to help Emily and I, we're family, and he accepted Jonathon and 80s Dave on our recommendation, but others? Butty has always been a loner, preferring his own company over that of others. If it wasn't for me and Emily coming over to see him he probably wouldn't interact with anyone if he could help it.

Actually, now I think about it, that is probably why he's been praying for a zombie apocalypse all these years. The human race would become largely wiped out and he could live his life in peace without having to deal with other people's needs and hang ups. Butty has enough trouble dealing with his own eccentricities never mind those of others. That's why he joined A.R.S.E. It was a way for him to communicate without meeting people face to face and he didn't have to be himself. To other A.R.S.E. members he was Lone Wolf, alien spotter and all round cool mutha fucker! To everyone else, he was the crazy lunatic that kept himself to himself. Well he got his wish, kind of. Zombies are here but he's not alone and personally I think having Dave, Jonathon, Emily and I around will do him the world of good and who knows, maybe he'll even start to enjoy the company of others. If not then there's a good chance he'll completely flip and we'll be added to his heads on spikes collection.

"You've done a fantastic job Sky Watcher, just like I told you. Keep me up to date with how things develop at your end. Any problems let me know and remember what I said, if you find you're in a spot of bother just ask yourself "What would Lone Wolf do?" Over and out Sky Watcher," Butty said before turning off the C.B. radio.

"So how many people are you in contact with using this old thing?" I asked, slapping the top of the C.B. radio with the palm of my hand which was met with a stern look from Butty.

Honestly, you think I'd eaten his last Rolo.

"Since the outbreak? Let me see, well there's Sky Watcher and Trust No One but he's been quiet for a while now. I haven't heard anything from the other Spotters. I suppose they didn't make it," Butty replied.

"At least we know there are others out there like us, surviving this thing," I said.

"There are a lot more that you might think, which brings me to the other reason I brought you up here," my brother said, walking to the skylight and opening the window, "Come and see for yourself"

I joined my brother at the skylight and climbed up on top of tins of spam to peer out of the window. From my elevated position, I looked out over the Weston Point area of Runcorn. Weston Point is a large housing estate containing schools, shops, pubs, a sports club and oh, the biggest incinerator and chemical plant you have ever seen. The chemical plant in particular is enormous and at night when brightly lit, resembles a large futuristic city Think of the opening sequence to Blade Runner, only bigger!

The time was just past 5am and it was a dark morning. With the power still operational, street lights illuminated the area and it was an eerie sight. Zombies slowly meandered, stumbling under street lights, casting large horrific shadows against houses and along roads. The one thing I noticed amidst the darkness and pockets of light was that the zombies were all heading in the same direction. I lifted my gaze and looked further afield to where the deaders were going. It appeared that the destination of the dead was the Pavilions; a large social club surrounded by sports fields.

"Use the telescope," Butty said.

I placed my eye to the viewfinder to see that my brother had the telescope positioned perfectly on the Pavilions. A large group of survivors looked to have been working through the night to secure the building. Men were atop ladders, boarding up windows whilst others protected the building from the increasing numbers of oncoming zombies. In front of the building, sprawled across the sports fields lay the fallen, both human and zombies alike. A bloodied battle between the dead and the living had raged through the night and the remaining survivors were protecting the building with their lives. It wasn't looking good. No matter how many zombies they would slay, others would soon follow and they would have to do it all over again. Moving my eye away from the viewfinder and looking out over the housing estate, it appeared that every zombie in Weston Point was heading towards them. If only the survivors could see what I could see then they would surely give up, lie down and let the fuckers eat them.

Although I admired their determination and will to survive, the future for these guys was looking bleak and nothing short of a miracle was going to save them from the army of undead heading their way.

"It's a massacre. How many people do you think are in there?" I asked.

"A few hundred to begin with would be my guess. But you only have to see how many of them are lying dead in the fields to see that's not the case now. They've been at it since yesterday afternoon. The Pavilions opened its doors as a place of refuge for anyone needing it but it didn't take long for things to turn to shit. I was watching events unfold whilst nailing zombie limbs to the house. My guess is that someone inside turned and all hell broke loose. Then of course there's the large gathering of fragrant human flesh all in one place. Every zombie in the area would be able to smell them. All those people together? It's like ringing a dinner bell for the undead. Give it a couple of hours and I reckon the coast will be clear for me and Dave to do a ciggy run. I know it sounds harsh but their misfortune is at our advantage. There's nothing we can do to save them so we might as well make the most of it. The streets will be quiet soon and perfect for a bit of shopping," Butty said.

"You're both out of your minds. You have a walk in closest stacked with cartons of cigarettes and you want more, you've seen what it's like out there," I said, moving away from the skylight.

"Not want little brother, need. You know how many cigarettes he smokes. He's probably lying there now, fast asleep with a tab hanging from his mouth. Plus you know how much I hate sharing," he replied.

"Don't I just. I've still got a scar from when you threw a cricket ball at my head because I was using your bat," I said, rubbing the side of my head where the ball had hit.

"I bought that cricket bat for the sole purpose of protecting us from zombies and what were you doing? Playing cricket with that Chris Drake kid that lived up the road!" Butty complained.

"So I was. I've not thought about Chris for years. I wonder how he is," I said.

"Well given that he had more interest in playing cricket than preparing for the apocalypse I would say he's probably doing very badly. Luckily for you John, you have me as a brother. What would have happened if the undead Armageddon had happened whilst you were getting bowled out for a duck? Speaking of ducks, I've been meaning to ask, have you come across any yet?" Butty asked.

"Ducks? No, why?" I asked, completely puzzled at how quickly the conversation had shifted from the chaos at the Pavilions to cigarettes to cricket to ducks, but that's my brother for you. The cheese had slipped from his cracker years ago.

"Never mind, remind me to tell you later when everyone is awake. Come on then Little Brother. The day is young and there is lots of work still to do around here if we are to see this thing through," Butty said, climbing down the ladder and exiting his attic.

"Oh come on you know how early it is, can't we sleep for a few more hours?" I pleaded.

"There'll be plenty of time for sleeping when we're dead, which will be sooner rather than later if we don't finish off securing this house".

Fuck my life.

Supermarket Sweep

Steven Pritchard sat slumped against the shelving units of Poundland, crunching his way through chocolate covered Brazil nuts as loud as he could but it was no good. Even wearing his fluffy pink ear muffs he could hear the hellish noise of zombies banging against the windows. It had been twenty seven hours since he and Tin Tin fortified themselves inside the discount store, securing the premises by locking all entrances and exits then piling up shop fittings in front of the window as extra protection. It had been a difficult night for Steven. Unable to remove the image of the woman he loved turning into a zombie, the death and transformation of Jess Smith repeated over and over in his head. It hadn't been easy, but the Battle for Poundland had been won by the living and since the victory, the moans and groans of the deaders outside had gradually increased as the hours passed and he couldn't help but think it wouldn't be long before he and Tin Tin would have to do battle once again. But for now ear muffs and the crunch of discounted chocolate coated Brazil nuts was all he had to drown out the frightening sounds of zombies as they relentlessly pounded on the front of the store.

"Nothing is airing, even the emergency broadcast has stopped," said Tin Tin dejectedly. "I'll try another one," he added, pulling the wrapping apart from another wind up radio.

Discarded radios and packaging surrounded Tin Tin. Having spent the last few hours trying desperately to find a channel still broadcasting, his demeanour had changed considerably compared to a day earlier when his quick thinking and will to survive had been instrumental in securing his and Steven's safety. A night of no sleep listening to the haunting sounds of the undead had taken its toll. Securing themselves inside Poundland had at first seemed like the perfect way to wait out the zombie outbreak. That is until Tin Tin completed a store inventory and realised that the shelves were not stacked with much in the way of useful products. Food wise there was chocolate, crisps, cereal bars, tinned hot dogs, powdered soup, and packs of processed meat - all of which were close to their use by date, lacking in nutrition and more importantly, in numbers. He had estimated that if they rationed what they had then the food supplies would last 5 weeks at the most. Fluids? 4 weeks at the most, just as long as they could stomach drinking nothing but sickly low budget energy drinks. Still, there were plenty of painkillers in stock to help numb the caffeine headaches.

"She's out of my life..." Steven sung with a mouth full of chocolate confectionery.

"Are you listening to me Steven? I said nothing is broadcasting," Tin Tin complained.

"She's out of my life..." Steven continued.

"Great, just great. We've got zombies up our arseholes, enough food and drink to last a month if we're lucky and you're mourning a woman you were too nervous to say hello to never mind ask out on a date," Tin Tin complained, throwing a wind up radio to the floor in frustration.

"I don't know whether to laugh or cry..." Steven warbled.

"One more note from you and I swear you'll regret it," Tin Tin threatened.

"I don't know whether to live or die..." Steven continued, his eyes now closed whilst nutty, chocolate chunks flew from his mouth as he sang.

"Right that's it..." Tin Tin fumed, leaning forward to lift an ear muff from Steven's head and yell "ZOMBIES EVERYWHERE, ARGH STEVEN HELP, ZOMBIES, ZOMBIES, ZOMBIES!"

Steven jumped to his feet in fright, screamed in fear then ran head first into the shelving unit opposite him, knocking boxes of cereal bars onto the floor.

"Bloody hell Tin Tin there was no need for that, you scared the shit out of me," Steven said, his heart pounding.

"No need? I didn't save your arse yesterday so I can spend the rest of the apocalypse listening to you crying over a woman you hardly knew and as for that singing... I bet you the rest of that bag of chocolate Brazil nuts that there're zombies outside with hands over their ears. In fact, I bet that's what all the moaning is we can hear. It's not because they want to eat us but because they want you to stop fucking singing!" Tin Tin said.

Firmly put in his place, Steven did not dare reply, fearing a response would only infuriate his friend more. Instead, he sheepishly lowered his head, picked up the cereal bars from the floor and replaced them on the shelving unit. He then stood quietly, staring at his shoes.

"Look mate I'm sorry I yelled down your ear. That was completely out of order. But we're in the shit here and you wallowing is not going to help the situation," Tin Tin said.

"Sorry Tin Tin I wasn't thinking. I just really miss her. For almost every day of the last 2 years I've stood at my till, looking out to the mobile phone shop opposite, watching Jess at work – watching her with customers, playing with her hair when she was bored and constantly spurning the unwanted advances of her slime ball boss. Before you say it again yes I know I have never spoken to her and the fact that I could never find the courage to tell her how I feel is tearing me apart," Steven said, tears filling his eyes.

"You are going to have to pull yourself together or it'll be something worse than sorrow that will be tearing you apart. We've got major problems here and I'm not sure what we're going to do. Whilst you've been sobbing your heart out, I've been assessing our situation and it's a lot worse than I thought it was going to be if I'm honest. Not only are we trapped in here with God knows how many zombies out front, we also have a very limited amount of food and drink. Sure we're fine right now but in a few weeks? And that's if the front of the shop holds out. If zombies continue to grow in numbers and push against the window the way they're doing then well, Steven my friend, we'll be fucked and your pretend girlfriend will be far from your mind when you are being eaten alive by the undead," said Tin Tin.

Steven walked towards the shelving units piled up against the window and entrance; the deathly groans of the undead increased in volume with every step.

"Do you really think they could break through?" Steven asked.

"There's every chance they'll break through. I don't think the glass used for the window came with a zombie proof guarantee but I'd say we're safe for now. I can't see anything getting in as it stands," Tin Tin replied.

Tin Tin had barely finished his sentence when a creaking sound filled the air followed by panelling dropping from the ceiling. Then suddenly and without warning, a man fell heavily to the floor landing between him and Steven. He was wearing a Halton Lea Shopping Centre security guard uniform and Tin Tin recognised him instantly as his colleague and friend Neil Gallagher.

Neil and Tin Tin had worked together for many years. It had been Neil that trained Tin Tin in his duties in how to catch a shop lifter whilst causing little disturbance, how to sense when trouble was brewing and how to keep calm in the most volatile of situations. Neil had taken his younger colleague under his wing and together they had worked hard to keep the shopping centre a relatively crime free environment.

"Please don't eat me!" Neil pleaded, lying motionless on the floor.

"Neil its Tin Tin, what the hell were you doing up there? It's good to see you. I was starting to think we were the only ones still alive in this place," Tin Tin said.

"Tin Tin? Man, am I glad to see you. Help me up will you, the fall has taken the wind out of me," Neil answered as his colleague helped him to his feet, "Thanks pal. I see you've barricaded yourself in here well enough and who's this you've got with you? Steven isn't it? I remember you. You're the guy that sits at his till all day staring at the girl who works in the mobile phone shop opposite. How long have you been here?"

Neil immediately got the impression that he may have said something he shouldn't have because Steven was now fighting back tears and walking away from the conversation to hide his obvious upset.

"Don't ask," Tin Tin said in response to Steven's obvious upset. "We've been here since yesterday morning. The first thing we did was secure this place. How about you?" Tin Tin asked.

"The same. I've been trapped inside Iceland with two of its employees. But the problem with Iceland is that almost all of the food is frozen so with nothing to cook anything in, no oven or microwave, we've not really eaten anything. Well, we've had some Pringles and ice cream but that's not exactly nutritional. The ice cream is a bugger to eat too. We have been using the plastic lids from boxes of Pringles as spoons. That's how I ended up dropping in on you guys. I figured I could navigate my way through the false ceiling that runs across each shop till I got to Wilko's. If it was zombie free I was going to liberate a microwave so we could cook up some real food," Neil replied.

Iceland is a British Supermarket specialising in budget frozen meals and the store had been part of Halton Lea Shopping Centre for many years. Neil had been running through the shopping mall when he was cut off by zombies blocking every exit. Luckily for him, he arrived at Iceland just as two of its employees were securing the shop and he managed to roll underneath the lowering metal security shutters just before they reached the floor. Neil's destination of Wilko's or Wilkinson as it is better known is a British retail store specialising in homeware and household goods.

"Real food? There's more nutrition in the cheap confectionery me and Steven have been eating than there is in the food from Iceland. There's nothing but low quality meat pumped full of water to make it look bigger and better than it actually is. No thanks. Anyway, Iceland is the last place you want to be. When the electricity fails, and it will, you'll be surrounded by thawing meat. The place will smell worse than the zombies," Tin Tin responded.

"Actually that isn't the real reason why I was crawling through the ceiling. I had no intention of taking a microwave or returning to Iceland. I just needed a story to get out of there. The two guys I was with are next to useless. They've done nothing but cower behind the frozen pizza section eating tub of ice cream after tub of ice cream whilst mumbling to themselves that the army will come and save us. Bloody useless. But you're a friend and a good one at that so I guess I can come clean. I was thinking that if Wilko's was zombie free, then I'd chance escaping through the doors at the back of the store that lead out to the car park. My car is there," Neil revealed.

"Escape? Are you crazy? There's no telling how bad it is out there. I mean, you can hear the noise from outside the shop right? There must be thirty to forty zombies trying to get to us and the numbers are rising. We've covered up the front windows and entrance so they can't see us but they just keep coming. It's like they somehow know we're in here," Tin Tin replied.

They all looked over to the front of the shop and listened to the undead moan and groan whilst slapping their hands against the glass front of Poundland.

"They can smell us," Neil replied.

"What did you say?" Tin Tin asked.

"Zombies. They can smell the living. It's the same over at Iceland. The metal shutters are down, the shop is secured and they can't see us but they still keep coming, crowding outside the entrance. The closer you get to them the louder they moan too. Here watch this..." Neil said, walking to the front of the shop.

The closer Neil got the louder the zombies groaned. He pressed himself up against the shelving barricade and the noise became unbearable.

"Please make it stop!" Steven pleaded, pushing his hands hard into the fluffy pink ear muffs still covering his ears.

"You see?" Neil said moving back towards Tin Tin. "They know we're here and more will come. It's only a matter of time before they force their way in. That's why I'm leaving. That and I need to see my family. You know my wife Kim is pregnant and my boy Conor... Christ if anything has happened to them I don't know what I'll do, I really don't. You guys should come with me. You can't hold out here forever. Come with me, we can go to my place. My brother

Shaun and his wife Linda live next door. We will be safe there I know we will. What do you say?"

"Let's say we do come with you and you're wrong? What if Wilko's has been compromised? What do we do then? Steven asked.

"We keep going. This is a big shopping centre. If we can't get out through Wilko's then we find another way. So what do you say? Are you guys in?" Neil asked.

"We're in," Tin Tin replied.

"Hey hang on a minute, I haven't agreed to anything," Steven moaned feeling pressured into committing to something he wasn't sure of.

Steven had never been the most decisive of people and he did not respond well to change. It was his indecisiveness that had led to a long and forgetful career as a Poundland checkout assistant. He had been given many opportunities over the years to change employment but had always declined. He was happy simply coasting along at the discount store, telling friends and family it was only temporary whilst he wrote his screenplay. The screenplay that was going to propel him to stardom and a new life away from Runcorn and from a job where he had to ask customers if they would like to buy a twin pack of out of date After Eight Mints for £1 every time they passed through the checkout.

"So you're going to stay here are you Steven? On your own singing soppy love songs to yourself, grieving over a girl you used to stalk, eating Brazil nuts just waiting for zombies to break through the shop window and tear you limb from limb?" Tin Tin said.

"Maybe," Steven said defiantly, moving to walk away.

As he turned, his foot slipped on a discarded wind up radio and he fell into the shelving barricade, bringing the unit crashing down, exposing the window and the forty plus zombies pressed up against it.

"Right well I'm in, when are we leaving, now? Give us a bunk up Tin Tin, I'll go first," Steven said, moving below the hole in the ceiling tiles where Neil had fallen, eager to leave following his accidental unveiling of the zombies at the window.

"Before we get going we should grab some bottles of water and maybe some of those cereal bars. They should be easy enough to carry without slowing us down. We'll need the fluids and energy. Don't worry fellas, we'll soon be out of here, trust me," Neil said.

Without the shelving units covering the window, the zombies became manic, ferociously pounding their hands and heads against the glass in relentless pursuit of the human flesh which was now on show. With the undead visible, Steven, Tin Tin and Neil felt compelled to move and move they did. After filling several Poundland carrier bags with food and drink supplies, they left the store by climbing on shelving and escaping through the hole in the roof, scurrying carefully along the false ceiling towards Wilko's.

Neil took the lead with Tin Tin and Steven following closely. Every slink and slither forward was done so with great care and precision. One wrong move and they would find themselves falling through the fragile ceiling panels to the floor below and, now they had moved past Poundland, what lay beneath was unknown. Still, they knew the shopping centre well and they knew how many shops they had to pass over before reaching their destination.

Crawling through electrical wires and thick dust, the trio continued over the betting shop and the slot machine casino until their painstakingly slow journey reached its end and they were finally above Wilko's with the sounds of panpipe music filling their ears.

"I think we're here," Neil whispered.

"No it's Wish You Were Here," Steven replied.

"What are you jabbering on about?" Tin Tin asked irritably.

"The music, it's panpipes Pink Floyd, listen…" he replied and then began to sing along to the music.

"How I wish, how I wish you were here,
We're just two lost souls swimming in a fish bowl, year after year,

Running over the same old ground,
What have we found?
The same old fears.
Wish you were here,"

"I friggin' don't wish you were here at the moment. I've already warned you once today about your singing," Tin Tin growled at Steven.

"Stop bickering you two and keep the noise down," Neil whispered.

Neil gently lifted a ceiling tile and peeked into the store below. Wilko's was fully illuminated with the bright lights revealing what appeared on first glance to be a zombie and human barren store. Directly below him was a wooden patio table and chair display. Just as Neil was about to tell the others that the shop looked safe for them to enter, the all too familiar noise of shuffling and groaning was heard over the mind numbing sounds of panpipes Pink Floyd.

"What do you see?" Tin Tin asked.

"A problem," Neil replied.

Shuffling into view came what was, just over a day ago, a young and fresh faced Wilko's employee by the name of Darren Gibbons. The past twenty four hours however, had not been kind on his complexion. His once pink skin was now a light grey with protracted dark veins clearly visible under his decaying flesh. Dried blood covered his mouth, neck and red employee shirt.

Darren was a popular member of the Wilko's team. His bubbly character was a hit with customers and he was always willing to go the extra mile when it came to customer care. He was liked by everyone… everyone but his manager that is. Sandra Looker took her job seriously and believed the key to a successful store was a regimental workforce and she saw his friendly demeanor as nothing more than a nuisance and a barrier between him and his day to day duties.

Neil watched as Darren slowly stumbled towards their location, stopping occasionally to sniff the air, using his decaying nose to catch the fresh human scent that Neil, Tin Tin and Steven had brought with them. The zombie store assistant let out a hellish groan and lifted his head to face the ceiling above. Neil quickly shut the tile.

"How well do you know the people that work in Wilko's?" Neil asked his companions.

"I don't, not really. Apart from Darren that is. He always stops by for a chat when he sees me. Lovely fella. I reckon if it wasn't for his nagging boss he'd spend all day chatting to people," Tin Tin replied.

"Well he's stopped by again, only this time he wants more than a chat," Neil replied.

Tin Tin lifted the ceiling tile to see the cold, dead face of Darren looking back at him who once again groaned towards the ceiling. The store assistant's mouth opened wide enough to give a clear view of his blue cracked tongue and beyond that his pale putrid throat.

Tin Tin had almost closed the ceiling tile when he heard the noise of objects being knocked from shelving units. He shifted his eyes to his left to see Darren's boss and nemesis Sandra Looker shuffling over to join her employee. She too was covered in dried blood from her mouth to her waist.

"Separated in life but together in death," he said to himself.

"What is it, what do you see?" Steven asked.

"Dead and hungry store assistant has now been joined by dead and hungry store manager. I don't suppose anyone remembered to bring any weapons or were we too busy bagging up cereal bars and energy drinks?" Tin Tin asked his companions whose lack of reply spoke volumes. "I didn't think so but luckily for us, I have a surprise in my trousers."

Steven and Neil's faces projected a look of both horror and surprise as Tin Tin reached inside his trousers and retrieved his trusted hammer - the same weapon that had been instrumental in securing Poundland a day earlier and it displayed the blood stains to prove it.

"You've crawled all the way from Poundland to here with that tucked down your trousers? That can't have been comfortable." Steven asked with a look of discomfort on his face.

"Yes I bloody did and a good job too as this hammer is the only defense we've got. Now, what I suggest is that you and Neil slowly lower yourselves... STEVEN!"

As Tin Tin was explaining his plan, the ceiling tiles underneath Steven broke away and he crashed heavily into the wooden garden furniture below. Through blurred vision he could see the zombies approaching and could hear his companions screaming for him to move but the fall had taken the wind out of him and no matter how hard he tried he could not rise to his feet. Instead he held his stomach in pain, rocking from side to side.

Darren, the zombie store assistant, had almost reached his intended target and with the meal in sight began his descent, leaning over the fallen Steven whilst gnawing his drool sopping mouth. The cold gloops of foul drool dripped from his mouth onto the back of his victim's neck.

Steven somehow found the strength to reach out his right arm finding a splintered wooden table leg from the broken garden furniture. With only seconds to spare before the teeth of the undead store assistant chewed into his exposed neck, he turned his body and with the table leg in hand, speared it through Darren's left eye. With the zombie dead he breathed a sigh of relief but much to Steven's dismay it wasn't over yet because now he had Sandra, Darren's boss and nemesis, to contend with.

He tried again to rise to his feet and this time managed to stand on one knee. On doing so, his blurred vision intensified and the room began to spin. He felt like he wanted to vomit and was uncertain of his surroundings. He was sure now that the fall not only winded him but had most likely given him a concussion. He shook his head swiftly in an attempt to clear the cobwebs but this only aided his symptoms. As the room started to spin, all he could do was watch as the swirling zombie moved closer towards him.

"Steven! Look at me, Christ man look at me!" Tin Tin screamed. "Focus on my face, don't try to look at the zombie, focus on me."

Trusting his friend, Steven looked up to the ceiling and concentrated hard on Tin Tin's face. At first he could see two faces but he scrunched his forehead and narrowed his eyes. Quickly the two became one and his vision returned.

"Are you good?" Tin Tin asked, to which Steven nodded a reply. "Then you better catch this."

Tin Tin dropped his hammer which Steven, to his own astonishment, caught expertly with both hands. In one fluid movement he stood on both feet, turned his body around and swung the weapon at Sandra. It was a perfect hit, fracturing the skull whilst sending her falling into the nearby shelving units. Wanting to make sure she was dead, he staggered over and repeatedly pelted the hammer into her face.

Looking over the puddle of blood, flesh, shattered skull fragments and dried out brain that used to be the head of the Wilko's store manager, Steven wiped away the beads of sweat that now seeped from his forehead. He needed a second to compose himself, to let his breathing return to its normal rate and to take stock of everything that had just happened. Then he staggered back to where he fell from the ceiling.

"Are you two coming or are you going to stay up there hiding like a pair of wimps?" said Steven who then fell to the floor and vomited heavily, "I knew I shouldn't have eaten all those chocolate coated Brazil nuts."

Steven's companions jumped down from the ceiling and joined him in Wilko's; Tin Tin offered his friend a drink and Neil surveyed the store. It appeared empty with the shutters at the front entrance stopping any zombies from entering. The automatic doors to the back of the store, leading to the car park and ultimately Neil's vehicle, also appeared secure.

"It looks like they were the only ones. There doesn't appear to be anyone else here, dead or alive," Neil informed.

"I wouldn't be so sure," Steven replied, wiping drips of energy drink from his mouth. "They both had dried blood around their mouths so they've eaten recently and someone must have secured the store."

"Maybe it was Darren and his boss that secured this place, they could have turned afterwards," Tin Tin offered.

"True, but that doesn't explain the blood. There must have been at least one other person with them, but I suppose there's nothing to worry about. They are probably dead now anyway," Steven replied.

"We should get moving, my car is just through the doors at the rear of the shop but first let's grab some tools to defend ourselves. I reckon the gardening and DIY sections are a good place to start," Neil suggested, rushing away to find some weapons.

"How are you holding up? That was a nasty fall man, you're lucky to be alive," said Tin Tin, placing an arm around his friend and helping him slowly walk away.

"I'll be honest mate I thought that was it, I really did. I felt I was going to die and for a moment there I gave in and was ready to meet my maker. Then I saw the zombie coming towards me and I thought fuck that shit, I want to live! Thanks for helping me focus and for the hammer. I got lucky grabbing the table leg for the first one but if it wasn't for you I would probably be zombie fodder right now. I'm ok though, really. It's nothing a few pain killers won't sort out," Steven replied.

"Well we're in the right place," Tin Tin replied, taking several boxes of strong painkillers from a nearby shelf. "I'll be keeping an eye on you though. You've more than likely suffered a concussion so no more zombie killing for the time being, leave that to Neil and me."

Tin Tin and Steven walked to the gardening aisle and were greeted by Neil stood statuesque with a shovel in hand looking directly ahead.

"Hey Neil, I dig the shovel! Get it? Dig the shovel?" Tin Tin smiled.

Neil didn't appear to appreciate the joke but he did acknowledge his friend's presence and pointed to what had taken his attention. Lying on the floor ahead of them was a pair of bloodied and torn legs; the rest of the body was obscured by a shelving unit. All three cautiously walked towards the legs with the extent of the injuries becoming clearer with every step. Steven gagged and quickly placed a hand over his mouth in an attempt to prevent further digested chocolate nutty confectionery from escaping. The legs were barely recognisable with muscle and skin almost completely stripped from bone. It was really only the shoes still covering the feet that gave them away as legs.

"Well I guess now we know where the blood came from. The three of them probably locked themselves in here hoping they'd be safe but two were already infected, turned and made a meal of the third. Poor bastard," Tin Tin surmised.

"Guys, you'll want to see this," said Neil, who had walked ahead to the other side of the shelving unit.

Steven and Tin Tin joined him to see that the upper torso of the body was missing and in its place lay a trail of blood leading away from the legs and out of sight. They followed the blood until finally they found the missing torso and it was not what any of them were expecting.

The upper torso stopped dragging itself and lifted its head upwards, sniffing the air intently. It then turned its putrid head to face them. It was female and was wearing a Wilko's uniform.

"Well you were nearly right Tin Tin. She must have turned whilst Darren and his boss were busy ripping her stomach apart. I guess zombies don't eat other zombies," Neil said, gripping his newly acquired shovel.

He walked towards the zombie which tried to meet him half way by dragging her torn body towards him. Using the shovel he swung hard, smashing the side of her head and flipping what remained of the body over onto its back. He lifted the shovel high, readying himself to drive it through her brain when his eyes caught her employee name badge. It read Debb Morris.

"Sorry Debb," he said before thrusting the shovel through her head, cracking the skull and pushing into her brain. "Please tell me killing zombies gets easier after you've put down your first one," he asked Steven and Tin Tin who both shook their heads in response.

The three of them walked towards the rear exit of the store, stopping only in the hardware section where Steven helped himself to a crowbar and Tin Tin replaced his hammer with a bigger sturdier model which he then used to smash through the window panels of the automatic doors. They exited to the car park and walked towards Neil's car, a silver Chevrolet Matiz. He could hear Tin Tin and Steven sniggering behind him.

"Before you say anything it's the wife's car, mine is in the garage," Neil tried to explain, worried that he would lose man points.

"Listen, I'm heading home to Weston Point. I can drop you anywhere you want to go just as long as it's not too out of the way or, if you like, you can stay with me. There's plenty of room at my house for you guys. It's completely up to you," Neil said.

Both Steven and Tin Tin gave each other the smallest of glances. It was all they needed to make up their minds. Neither of them had much in the way of family, with only their parents living in Runcorn. That one small glance was enough to show that they both felt the same. They would both take not knowing if their parents were alive over returning home to find them dead, or worse.

"We're staying with you, we're stronger together but there's one thing you need to understand," Tin Tin spoke in a quiet and serious voice. "As long as you are driving that car, Steven and I have the right to take the piss out of you relentlessly, no matter how many zombies you kill along the way."

"Hey I told you, it belongs to my wife!" Neil protested.

They entered the vehicle and took their seats. Neil driving, Tin Tin in the front passenger seat and Steven choosing to lie down in the back - the effects of his concussion demanded he did so. Neil wanted nothing more than to be home with his pregnant wife and young son. His body ached with the fear that something had happened to them. Steven and Tin Tin were more than willing to help him get home. They both believed that staying together would be considerably more desirable than going their separate ways.

Or so they thought...

Journal Entry 9

Whilst the rest of the house slept, my brother sent me swinging down the dreaded rope ladder that hung from the spam store room window, leading to the front of the house. The same place where a day earlier, Butty had killed and chopped up five members of the ever increasing undead population, nailed their body parts to the house then placed their putrid decaying heads on spikes outside his front door. Why he had sent me out front I wasn't too sure but, armed only with a meat cleaver, I gingerly clambered down the ladder and waited for him as instructed. With morning sunlight quickly infiltrating the lessening darkness, I looked properly upon the faces of the spiked heads for the first time and they were indeed the people my brother had described. I found myself transfixed, unable to move my eyes from their pale, disgusting faces. The zombies I had encountered up to this point had all been mobile and, after they had been disposed of, I never felt the need, or indeed had the opportunity, to stick around. But now I had the chance to study their faces in detail.

A white glaze covered the eyes belonging to the cold, putrefying heads of the undead, the iris and pupil being no longer visible. Covering gaunt and sunken features, the skin appeared thin and grey of colour. It's no wonder I had not recognised them on first viewing. This infection, disease, sickness or whatever you want to call the cause of the zombie outbreak had quickly ravished and twisted the once pink, living flesh that belonged to the people I had been privileged to call friends. Standing out there on my own with the heads of my dead pals for company was terrifying and I had never felt so alone. Then without warning a harrowing wind whistled through the leaf deprived trees that surrounded the front of my brother's house, swiftly followed by the sound of broken twigs snapping below heavy footsteps. I gripped the meat cleaver tight and nervously moved backwards, walking between the row of spiked heads and placing my back up against the house. Whatever was coming, I wanted to be in the best position to defend myself.

As the heavy, clumsy sound of shuffling feet dragging along the ground got closer and the groans that now accompanied it became louder, the knot in my stomach tightened. I was alone and, unless the rotting zombie heads planted on top of the spikes in front of me were about to magically spring back to life and offer some much needed tactical advice, I was going to go with the one plan I had which was to run at the fucker and hack away at the dead bastard's head as fast and as hard as I could. Only, I didn't have chance to put my plan into action as just as I was about to attack, my brother shuffled his size nines around the corner of the house holding several large wooden stakes whilst doing his best zombie impression.

"Fuck sake Butty you nearly got a meat cleaver through your head you crazy shit!" I yelled.

"Brilliant, I knew it would shit you up. That's why I sent you out here on your own. As for the meat cleaver, I know you John, there is no way you would have attacked without getting a good look first. You wouldn't risk killing someone living, you'd make sure they were dead first," Butty said.

"Well try a trick like that again and I might just make an exception. What are you carrying anyway and where did you come from? You never came down the rope ladder?" I asked.

"Of course I didn't. It's a bloody death trap that thing. I climbed down a retractable ladder from my bedroom window around the back of the house. As for what I'm carrying… Something every man should never leave the house without - protection. Come with me and I'll show you why I dragged you out here at this ungodly hour," he said.

Really, a retractable pissing ladder and he made us climb that 'death trap' as he put it only the night before. I'm sure he does stuff like this for his own amusement.

We walked away from the front of the house to the steep stone steps leading up to Weston Road and where 80s Dave had parked the Ford Thunderbird. It was difficult to see anything from our lowered position such was the extent of the overgrowth. Even without greenery the mass assortment of leafless trees and bushes was enough to obstruct our view of the road above almost completely.

"When this was Nan and Granddad's house they never would have let the front garden get in this state. Granddad used to be out here every day weeding and tending to his flowers. Now look at it," I said.

"Beautiful isn't it. Absolutely perfect. For years you've been moaning at me to sort it out and let's just say that I had. What would you see now?" Butty asked.

"I don't know. A lovingly cared for garden with no overgrowth? Or even just a freshly cut lawn. Anything would be better than this," I replied.

When our grandparents passed away they left everything to Butty and me. I got the money, which I used to buy a home to raise Emily, and Butty was left their house. That was thirteen years ago and my brother had not so much as watered a plant since. In his neglect, the once picturesque and lovingly tendered garden was now more like a jungle than anything, or it would be if it were summer. At this time of year, deep into winter, it was a mass of knotted and tangled twigs and branches.

"No overgrowth? Without the overgrowth we would be exposed and I don't just mean to zombies but survivors also. These are desperate times we're living in John. A house this big... it would not take long for someone to take their chances and try to loot the place. Or worse, a group of survivors could try to take it for themselves. Then where would we be? Fighting the living as well as the dead and that's the last thing we need. This overgrowth is camouflage. Just like the rotting undead body parts stuck to the walls are hiding us from zombies by masking our scent, these bushes and trees hide the house from other survivors. And you thought I was being lazy all these years when in fact I was doing what I've always done. I was preparing for the apocalypse," Butty said, puffing his chest out with pride as if he had worked hard to create a garden Alan Titchmarsh wouldn't want to tackle.

Once again he was right. Thirteen years of neglect had indeed created enough overgrown bushes, brambles and trees to camouflage the house. One day the nutty bastard will be wrong and I hope to God I'm there to piss on his chips when he is.

"Grab a wooden stake little brother, this is the plan. Nailing zombie parts to the house is working so far but it's a task that needs to be repeated every couple of days. Rain, wind, snow, cold... they are exposed to the elements 24/7 and need to be kept fresh. So we need a plan B should plan A fail and the zombies pick up our meaty scent. Now the path down to the house is steep and from what we know, co-ordination isn't something the undead possess. My guess is that, should they attack from the front, they wouldn't have the ability to successfully manoeuvre down the pathway and would no doubt fall flat on their rotting arses. Even more likely is that they will ignore the path all together and just come tumbling over the wall, falling into the overgrowth. If that happens, I suspect the twisted, tangled twigs and branches would contain a few of them but not many and that's where these stakes come in. We're going to hammer them into the ground. Some pointed vertically and others on an angle. Should zombies come plunging over the wall then they'll be met with a stake through the chest or whichever body part the wooden spike penetrates. For those that survive the fall the other stakes that we place on an angle should take care of them. It won't kill them of course just trap them and that leaves us with the simple task of strolling over and smashing their brains in. Easy! Let's get started with these and then I'll get the other fifty I've got stored around the back of the house," Butty said.

"Fifty? Christ Butty I'm recovering from a bad back, what are you trying to do, cripple me?" I moaned.

"Don't worry little brother, I don't expect us to do it all by ourselves, just to make a start that's all. It'll soon be time for me and Dave to go on the ciggy run so you can get Emily and Jonathon to finish things off. I'm sure they won't mind. In fact, it was Emily that helped me make all the stakes. She's a good kid is our Emily," Butty said.

I've said it before and I'll no doubt say it again, I really do need to limit the amount of time my brother spends with

Emily. She should be spending her free time with her friends. Not concocting plans to zombie proof the house with her crazy Uncle Butty. Then again, these days her only friends are Jonathon and 80s Dave. Shit she's doomed!

We spent the next hour hammering wooden stakes into the ground. It was exhausting work and unfortunately for me, the pain in my back had returned with force. It felt like someone had reached inside my skin and grabbed hold of my back muscles then violently started twisting and squeezing. Butty was like a machine, hammering stake after stake into the ground, stopping occasionally to cast his crazy judgemental eye over to my progress only to *'tut'* and shake his head at how little work I had done. After the fifth or sixth disapproving glance from my brother I chose to ignore him. I was trying my hardest to keep up and thought I was doing a bloody good job considering my injury. Plus, I had more important things on my mind than seeking my brother's approval, like what I had seen earlier through the window in his attic.

Images of those poor people trapped at the Pavilions had been playing heavily on my mind. Whether they knew it or not they were done for. Every zombie in Weston Point was heading their way and there was nothing we could do to help them. I felt helpless. Looking through my brother's telescope I had witnessed the struggle those people had and still were experiencing at the hands of the undead. The fields surrounding the Pavilions were scattered with victims, both human and zombie alike, products of the bloodied battle that had raged through the night. Unfortunately for the survivors, for every zombie slain, more were waiting in line. It was a never ending fight and one they couldn't win. Not on their own anyway. But who could help? There was nothing we could do, that was for sure. Any attempt to assist from our little band of survivors would be certain suicide and I for one had no interest in putting myself or my family's lives in danger. I'm including Jonathon and 80s Dave in that statement because that's what they were to me now, family. Jonathon being my daughter's boyfriend had become the closest thing to a son-in-law I was likely to have and Dave, well, he is quite possibly the only friend I have left that isn't dead or undead and he means as much to me as Emily and Butty.

Talking of Dave, it was whilst struggling to hammer stakes into the ground that a strong whiff of cigarettes filled my nostrils.

"Morning Ace, what the fuck are you doing outside? It's freezing and this window's letting a draft in. I'm so cold my nipples look like blueberry muffins!" Dave shouted, puffing on a cigarette whilst leaning out of the window I had climbed down from earlier.

"What does it look like I'm doing? I'm helping my crazy brother zombie proof the house," I replied.

"I heard that," Butty groaned, hammering in another stake.

"Helping? From up here lar it looks like you're slowing him down. You get yourself back in the house and make us a brew and I'll take over down there. If we leave you to it you won't be finished in time for the next apocalypse never mind this one," Dave said, making to climb down the rope ladder.

"Stay where you are Dave, Emily and Jonathon can finish off down here. We've got a ciggy run to go on and I know just the place. Go and get yourself ready, I'll be up in a minute," Butty said, hammering in the last stake of his shift and wiping the sweat from his brow.

"Ready when you are kidda," Dave said, throwing the remainder of his cigarette out of the window, the lit tip singeing the decapitated manky and rotting head of my former neighbour and topless sunbather Paula Brownrigg.

My brother walked past the rope ladder, gave it a disapproving glance then turned to me and muttered "Bloody death trap," before disappearing from view, turning the corner to the back of his house. Well I was damned if I was going to let him leave me on my own again and climbing the rope ladder was out of the question, so I hobbled after him. The putrid smell of the undead became stronger with every laboured step. The closer I got to the back of the house the more intense the stench became. It was then I remembered my conversation with Butty from earlier where he detailed how many zombies he had killed. I knew this wasn't going to be pretty and I was right.

My brother's back garden was large and long with the far end reaching into Weston Point. He had built an 8ft wooden fence many years ago, adding security to his property whilst also cutting off any access from the estate. Now, Butty had told me he had spent the best part of last week preparing the house in anticipation of the apocalypse but what he had done with the garden was incredible. He had raised the height of the fence by a further 5ft. The new layer to the fence was dripping in grease paint and on the top he had placed broken glass. Realising the house was vulnerable from the rear, his main intention here was to keep out unwanted guests of the human kind. As an extra security measure, Butty had constructed a secondary fence made from chicken wire. Tied to the chicken wire, hung many pots and pans. Should anyone make it over the first fence unharmed they would not make it over the second fence unheard.

The garden fortress only served to distract me momentarily from the horror walled within it. In the middle of the garden lay a pile of dead zombies. Well I say pile. It was more like a mountain! There must have been close to fifty in the large deathly heap, the mangled and rotting bodies of the dead entwining with each other making it difficult to see where one zombie ended and another began. It was the stuff of nightmares and the smell, my God; it made a slaughterhouse smell like the Chelsea Flower Show in comparison.

I looked to my brother who was climbing the ladder to his bedroom window.

"I told you not to look in the back garden," he said, watching as I bent down and spewed out the contents of my stomach.

You know what? Once again the fruit loop was right!

Avenging Angel

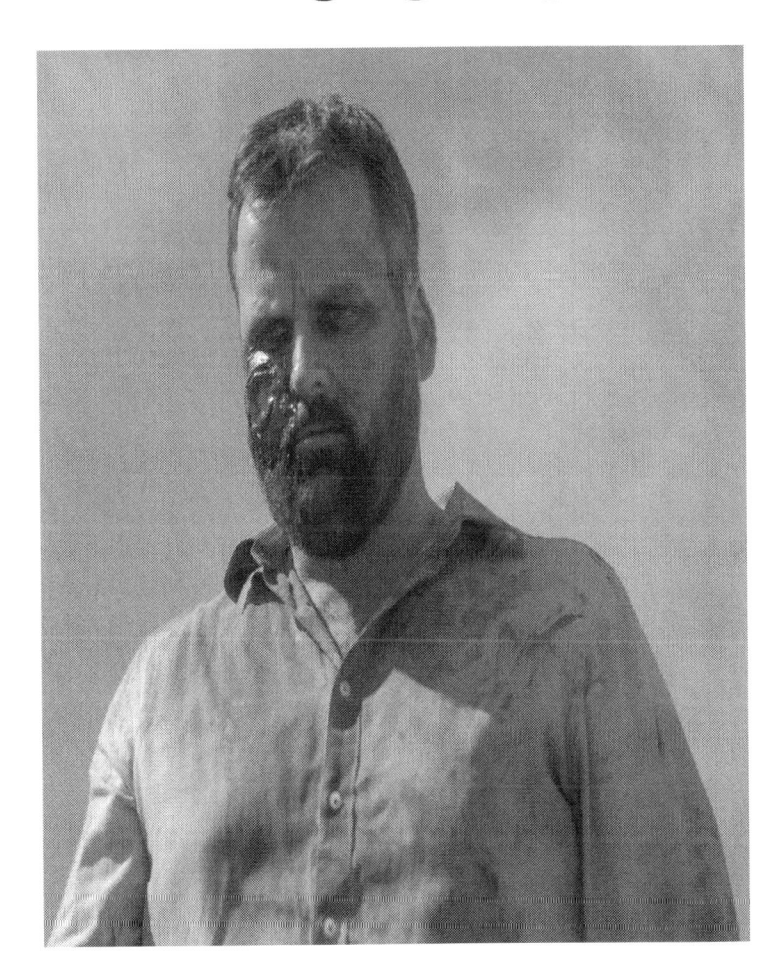

Melany Brunka had been flicking through television channels all night. It was 12 hours since broadcasts stopped but still she continued to press the channel button on her remote control, hoping for news that the zombie outbreak was over and maybe the army had been called in to clear the infected from her town.

She turned on her radio. The emergency broadcast from Halton FM that had repeated since the previous morning played through the speakers. It was telling her to go to the Pavilions if she needed shelter. Shelter she had; it was her boyfriend Rod that was missing.

Rod, a keen cyclist, was in training for his second Coast to Coast challenge, a journey that would take him the length of England in two days to raise money for Halton Haven Hospice. He left his house early the previous morning for a bike ride before going to work. He never returned. When she awoke to see the streets filled with the living dead and Rod nowhere to be seen, she believed him to be hiding somewhere, waiting for a chance to return home. Little did she know he lay dead in Heath Road Medical Centre, his head bashed into a bloodied pile of broken bone and brains.

Mel spent her time torn between the television and the door to her home. Every news report told her to stay indoors but Rod was gone and she struggled deeply with what she knew to be the safe thing to do and what her heart compelled her to do. She ran to the front door stopping short of opening it. Slowly her hand reached for the lock, an action she had repeated many times since yesterday.

Closing in on the lock, her reach appeared to act as a volume control for the zombies outside. The closer she came to opening the door the louder the moans and groans of the undead. With her hand now on the latch, the sounds became deafening. She quickly withdrew, unable to withstand the noise any longer, and returned to the living room, taking her place in front of the television. If she was to do as her heart compelled then she needed help, lots of it. She needed the Box of Doom.

The Box of Doom was a large wooden chest containing left over alcohol from when her friends would visit. Usually it contained the kind of booze nobody wants to drink. Culprits such as ouzo, Drambuie, cheap wine and Pernod would always be present. But there was also the good stuff too. Vodka, Gin, Malibu and Crème De Cacao plus a selection of cocktail mixers were always there to complete The Box.

Mel retrieved The Box from her kitchen, placed it on the floor and opened the lid, unleashing its distinctive boozy smell. No bar, not even a tramps vest, smelt like the Box of Doom when opened. The alcoholic aroma filled her nostrils and the fumes alone made her head spin. If she felt tired from being up all night she was certainly awake now. The smell emanating could wake a hibernating bear. She reached inside and removed an almost empty bottle of Vodka, the favourite tipple of her friend Sarah Layton. She removed the top and raised it high, proposing a toast to her friend.

"Here's to you Sarah," she said, downing the remaining vodka.

She couldn't have known but her friend was lying dead in a crashed Boeing 747 not a fifteen minute walk away.

With the vodka now gone, she reached inside once more and retrieved a half drunk litre bottle of Gin. It was her friend Julia Kelly's tipple of choice and next on Mel's drinking list. She removed the top and raised the bottle high.

"For you Julia," she toasted then with one hand pinching her nostrils closed, she gulped down the gin quickly in an attempt to halt the harsh taste hitting the back of her throat.

Julia would have been proud of her friend's toast, if her zombiefied body was not currently lying dead in a sea of shower gel outside Poundland.

With the room beginning to spin, she again reached inside The Box and removed a near full bottle of Rum, the preferred drink of her friend Debbie Barlow. With one more toast to go she raised the bottle high into the air.

"Debbie! Down the hatch!" she said.

Mel took a long swig of rum, filling her with a comforting warmth which was in contrast to Debbie's frozen body that lay floating beneath the thin ice of the River Mersey.

Taking the rum with her, she approached the living room window and pulled back the curtains. Zombies were everywhere. Swaying, shuffling and sniffing the air occasionally whilst releasing hellish groans. She closed the curtain over, not ready to see anymore. Drinking on its own was not going to be enough and if she was to find courage to leave and look for Rod then she needed a weapon and a way of protecting herself. If only, like in the comics and movies they both loved, she was a superhero. Then she could rid this cursed world of the undead and restore normality.

She took another long drink of rum. As alcohol enhanced the warm fuzziness filling her body a flame ignited. A flickering light of an idea began to burn. She knew what she needed to do.

With rum in hand she ran upstairs and opened the door to the spare bedroom. Both Mel and Rod were keen collectors. Comic books, movie and TV memorabilia... anything attached to the things they loved they would collect and it all went into the spare room. It was a geek's paradise and Mel in particular loved spending time in there, organising and adding to her Marvel, DC, Star Wars and Star Trek collectables. It was these items that triggered her most awesome of ideas.

60 minutes had passed since Mel entered the room. If her neighbours had still been alive they would have complained about the loud banging and moving of units followed by screams of joy when she located the items needed. But now, after an hour of preparation, she was ready and emerged from the spare room, not as Melany Brunka but as Apocalypse Girl, ready to kick every rotting zombie's ass that stood in her way.

Covering her feet were her trusted Dr. Martens boots, the same pair she had owned since she was sixteen years old. They were tough as old nails and capable of crushing the head of any zombie looking to be stomped into the ground.

On her legs she wore black combats which were covered with pockets filled with replica Batman throwing stars, made famous from the Dark Knight Trilogy. They had been a drunken late night eBay purchase, something that happened all too often in Apocalypse Girl and Rod's household and accounted for 40% of the spare room's content.

Around her waist, adding to the DC comics theme, she wore an original Batman TV show replica utility belt, yellow in colour and perfect for carrying essentials such as medical supplies, food and water. But more importantly it also carried a full size prop sword from the movie Braveheart and a Star Wars purple Lightsaber.

On her upper body she wore her official Star Trek Next Generation Science / Medical Officer uniform complete with Commander pips.

She had placed her left hand inside a large green Incredible Hulk fist. Made from hard plastic it was capable of delivering a brutal strike without sustaining damage.

Covering her right hand she wore a Darth Vader replica glove, purely for aesthetic reasons as she thought it was fucking cool but what her hand gripped was the weapon to end all weapons. Feared throughout the Galaxy as an instrument of death, Apocalypse Girl reasoned that zombies would probably die just from looking at it, for in her right hand she wielded a full size Klingon Bat'leth. The Bat'leth is a curved long sword with four sharp points and a gripping handle on the back. Like a martial arts weapon in style it became part of popular culture after first appearing in the TV show Star Trek Next Generation. Known as an effective weapon, laws on ownership of a Bat'leth differ from country to country and have been known to be used in martial arts competitions as well as for acts of crime.

Clipped around her neck and flowing over her back was a Superman cape. She'd had it custom made and instead of an 'S' as in the Man of Steel's family crest there was a 'B' for the House of Brunka. Finishing off her outfit was a red teenage Mutant Ninja Rafael mask covering her eyes.

She took one last drink from the bottle of rum then placed it into her utility belt. She was ready to find Rod and in the process kick some zombie ass!

She exited her house and surveyed the scene. The undead appeared to be everywhere, shuffling in every direction. Several of the nearby deaders shifted their heads, picking up her scent. Before she knew it they were at the wall that separated the road from the small garden in front of her house. It had taken over twenty four hours and plenty of alcohol to summon the courage to leave her home. She was damned if she was going to retreat back inside now.

"IT'S CLOBBERING TIME!" screamed Apocalypse Girl.

She rushed forward and placed a well-aimed Hulk fist square in the face of the nearest zombie, sending it hurtling backwards, knocking several of the others down like a deathly row of dominos.

"Awesome!" she exclaimed.

Using her Hulk fist for leverage she jumped the wall, booting a zombie hard in the middle of the face, propelling it backwards to join its undead friends on the ground. Her beloved Dr. Martens did not let her down and the tough boot exterior, combined with the force of the kick, shattered the zombie's nose leaving only a hole where the nostrils used to be.

"Apocalypse girl SMASH!" she growled, stomping her boots through the heads of every fallen zombie.

STOMP, STOMP, STOMP, STOMP, STOMP!

She checked her surroundings; every zombie close by was eliminated. Hulk fist placed on her hip and Bat'leth held high she stood victorious, both of her boots resting in zombie brains. But there was no time to celebrate her triumph. She had to stay focused. She had to find her boyfriend.

Remembering Rod's cycle route she ran in the direction of Dukesfield, a housing estate situated close to the Runcorn Bridge, pausing momentarily to take in its destruction.

"Holy fucking spitballs!" she said, mouth open, watching as the Runcorn half of the bridge broke free and dropped into the River Mersey.

She now knew what the horrendous deafening rumble was she had heard a day earlier. Something large had fallen from the sky and destroyed the Runcorn Bridge. She had to see what caused this destruction and turned right on to Waterloo Road, past All Saints Church before turning onto Mersey Road. There she saw the crashed Boeing 747 and in front of it two men fighting a gaggle of crazed geese and ducks. One man, with a heavily bruised face was having his ankles nipped by a small duck coated with blood stained feathers. The other man, who was wearing a leopard print fake fur coat, swatted and thwarted the deranged animals away with a walking stick. She contemplated helping but the man in the fur coat looked to have things under control and Apocalypse Girl had more important matters to attend to.

She turned to run back along Waterloo Road but was faced with two zombies stumbling towards her. She looked to her Klingon Bat'leth for protection.

"Hegh zombie Veqlargh!" she barked at the zombies in her best Klingon, then with one swipe of the Bat'leth, removed both of their heads.

Apocalypse Girl was not expecting the Bat'leth to be so effective and in her joy performed a little dance, doing the running man whilst singing "Oh Yeah! Oh Yeah! Oh Yeah!" again and again.

Even in her darkest moments she was always a good drunk.

Another victory and she was starting to believe. Believe that she had a chance against the undead and in her ability to find Rod and find him alive.

Time to move and running towards Dukesfield, keeping an eye on the many zombies that roamed close by, she made the decision to find a vehicle. It was too slow and dangerous to continue on foot, even if she was turning out to be a tough ass zombie slayer.

She stopped under the arches of the Runcorn railway bridge which crossed the River Mersey and was positioned alongside the Runcorn Bridge. She was surprised to see it in one piece but that was not the reason she stopped. Directly ahead was a small girl standing in the road, wearing a night gown and hugging a teddy bear close to her chest. Apocalypse girl approached cautiously.

"What's your name little girl?" she asked.

"My name is Heather Nicholls," said the little girl, lifting her head to reveal her eyes filled with tears.

"Why are you out here alone? Do you have anyone looking after you?" Apocalypse Girl asked.

"My mum is inside, there is a man trying to eat her," Heather replied, looking to her home.

Apocalypse girl turned to the house she referred to. An end terrace town house with broken windows and an open front door. Torn between the need to find her boyfriend and help the little girl she looked along the road in the direction her mission was taking her. She didn't have time for distractions but she could not leave this girl. She needed help and what kind of superhero would she be if she ignored this little girl's need?

"Come with me Heather, I will save your mum," Apocalypse Girl said, taking the little girl's hand.

They approached the open doorway and entered the house. In the hallway bloodied foot prints left a deathly trail up the stairway and moans of the undead could be heard.

Holding the Bat'leth in front of her she took to the stairway and motioned for Heather to stay in the hallway.

As more of the second floor came in to view, so did the zombie that was slapping its fists against the bathroom door. It was a tall thin man, naked apart from novelty Ghostbusters underpants which in green lettering read 'I ain't afraid of no ghost' across his pale dead bottom.

"Do you think the man is a zombie?" Heather whispered.

"Is the atomic weight of cobalt 58.9?" Apocalypse Girl replied, which was met with a confused expression.

The zombie stopped slamming up against the bathroom door and turned to face Apocalypse Girl, advancing towards her with saliva dripping from his thin lips and slithering down his blue gaunt chest. She swung the Bat'leth, slicing the zombie's neck, causing it to split and snap backwards. Hanging only by a fleshy thread, the zombie's head ripped free from the neck as the body fell to the floor. She walked over to the head which looked back at her, gnashing its teeth. Removing her Braveheart replica sword from her Batman Utility belt, she brought it down quickly, stabbing it through the centre of the forehead.

"They may take away our lives, but they'll never take away our FREEDOM!" she yelled, "It's safe for you to come out now," Apocalypse Girl said to Heather's mother who was hiding behind the bathroom door.

The bathroom door slowly opened and Heather's mother stepped out, looking frantically for her daughter.

"Heather!" She cried as her daughter ran up the stairway, skipped over the slayed zombie's body and jumped into her mother's arms.

"Die Jose Versluys!" She yelled, booting the zombie repeatedly. "That's Jose my neighbour. The creepy shit was always knocking at the house, asking to borrow daft things like a cup of milk or salt and he would stand there staring at me. Even when dead he couldn't leave me alone," she continued, putting in another boot for good measure, "How can I repay you?"

"I need a vehicle if you know of anything. It's too dangerous out there on foot," Apocalypse girl said.

"My friend Angie Parkes, her Mini Cooper is outside. You can take that," she replied.

"Won't your friend mind me taking it?" Apocalypse Girl asked.

"No she's dead," Heather's mum informed solemnly, "But that's the problem. She's not dead dead and she's sat inside it," came the reply.

"Look after your mum little one," Apocalypse Girl said to Heather, ruffling her hair before sliding down the stairway bannister, her red cape raising as wind rushed beneath it.

"Who was that girl, Heather?"

"A superhero, mummy."

Out on the street Apocalypse Girl approached the red Mini Cooper parked to the side of the house. In the driver's seat was a corpse - Angie, the friend that Heather's mum told her about. She appeared motionless through the frost covered glass of the vehicle. Using her cape, Apocalypse Girl wiped the frost from the driver's window, bringing her face close to the glass as she looked in to get a clear look at the body in the passenger seat then the corpse jerked its head suddenly, quickly turning to face Apocalypse girl whilst thrashing to and throw in its chair.

Looking through the window, she could see the keys to the vehicle resting in the ignition. Resisting temptation to smash through the glass with her Hulk fist, she quickly pulled on the handle and swung the door open, stepping away from the Mini Cooper and protecting herself with the Bat'leth. The zombie tried frantically to exit the car but the fastened seatbelt prevented its movement. Instead, it groaned and snapped its jaw, reaching out to its would-be victim.

Studying the zombie, Apocalypse Girl noted how angry and desperate it was to taste human flesh. Its actions reminded her of Rod first thing of a morning before drinking his coffee and she thought how maybe all the undead really needed was a strong brew and everything would be OK. She smirked to herself amused with the theory that a quick caffeine pick me up could bring the zombie apocalypse to an end. Then Rod stole her thoughts and urgency returned. No time for wistful ponderings. She needed that vehicle.

She opened the passenger door and sat inside, positioning herself directly behind the zombie. As it turned to face her, twisting its body so that its head poked through the gap between the driver and front passenger seats, she stabbed at it with the Bat'leth's sharp edged spike, piercing the forehead and penetrating its brain. The dead zombie slumped, dark congealed blood oozed from the stab wound to its head. Removing herself from the Mini, Apocalypse Girl pulled the zombie free from the driver's seat and took her place behind the wheel, slamming the door shut.

Turning the ignition key, Eye of the Tiger by Survivor boomed through the speakers. The owner of the car had been listening to the Rocky Soundtrack. How apt

Apocalypse Girl thought, as it was also Rod's favourite music to cycle to.

Possessing the Eye of the Tiger, she turned the volume up fully and revved the engine. Attracted by the noise, every zombie in the area descended upon the vehicle. At a slow steady pace she drove away. Like a pied piper for the dead they followed her as she lured them away from the home of Heather and her mother. She did this along every street in Dukesfield whilst taking care to look for signs of her boyfriend but there was none. In no time she had searched the whole estate and behind her had a following of over two hundred undead, all shuffling along to the inspirational sounds of the Rocky Soundtrack. She led them out of Dukesfield, along Egerton Road and onto Station Road with The Railway Pub in front of her.

Apocalypse Girl lowered the window and lent her head out, looking to the zombies behind her. In her best Mickey voice she yelled...

"What's a matter with ya? If ya wanna keep up with me you gotta crap thunder and eat lightning!"

Putting her foot down, she sped away towards Picow Farm Road and Balfour Street, leaving the undead behind her.

Time to make up lost ground.

Slowing down she surveyed the carnage ahead. Dead zombies and the ever present fallen birds covered Balfour Street. From the Co-Operative Supermarket to BJ & J Owens Newsagents, the road was barely visible below a carpet of dead walkers. Minis were not known for their suspension and as she slowly drove over the dead, she jostled about in her seat, her head bouncing from side to side. She felt the underneath of the car scrape against something large which caught against one of the rear wheels, bringing the Mini to a halt.

She lowered the car window and lifted her upper body out, looking to the undead covered road below her. Her heart almost stopped when she saw the black frame and red trim handle bars of her boyfriend's Boardman road bike pushed against the rear wheel of the vehicle. She quickly left the car and began inspecting every corpse littering the road but Rod was not there. A naked old woman and a one armed transvestite she could find but her boyfriend was not amongst the dead. She breathed a sigh of relief. Whatever happened here, he had got away but in which direction? He could be anywhere.

"Hel..., help meee."

She poised herself to attack, Hulk fist raised and Bat'leth ready to swing. Where did the voice come from? Balfour Street was awash with dead. Not a living person in sight. Then to her right, before the road opened up to another Street, she saw one of the many corpses on the ground begin to move, slowly shifting from side to side.

"Help... meee."

She approached with caution, treading carefully as she tip toed across the dead. Nearing the moving corpse, she noticed the body was not stirring unaided. There was someone trapped underneath.

A bloodied arm reached up from under the dead zombie.

"Don't leave me. I have a family. Pete, my name is Peter Beck, my wife she, she will be waiting for me, please…"

She moved the zombie with her boot to reveal a gore covered petrified male face. She reached down to grab the man's hand and pull him free but at the last moment noticed scratch marks running from his wrist to his elbow. The man noticed her looking at his arm.

"It's not a scratch, it's not, please, you can't leave me you can't…"

The man vomited heavily. Like a geyser from hell, puke sprayed into the air before falling and covering the dead that surrounded. Apocalypse Girl had the sense to anticipate the sick fountain and stepped back, out of its reach.

"Save me."

"I will."

Apocalypse Girl removed her Braveheart sword and thrust it downwards, straight through his forehead. Placing her boot on the head of the man, she pressed down with her foot and pulled hard on the sword, freeing it from his skull. After wiping her sword clean on a nearby dead zombie's clothing she took a long drink from her bottle of rum then made her way back to the Mini Cooper. That's when she heard the singing.

"Why do you build me up buttercup, baby,

Just to put me down and mess me around,

And worst of all, you do do do baby when you say you thing,

But I do de do..."

To her left, only a short walk from her location, a man singing could be heard coming from inside BJ & J Owens newsagents. Apocalypse Girl inspected the exterior of the shop, the 'NO ZOMBIES' graffiti on the window, the large pile of dead zombies outside and the 'Open' sign on the door. A strong smell of bleach filled her nose.

"I need you,

More than what's a ma thingy,

And do de da do from the start,

So build me up buttercup don't break my heart,"

She carefully opened the shop door and poked her head inside. There she saw Barry, the owner of the newsagent with mop in hand, cleaning a blood stained floor with a spring in his step and a song in his heart.

"If you're coming in shut the door behind you. You'll let a draft in never mind any zombies that might be close by. As you can see I've only just cleaned up after killing the last lot. Now then, what can I get you?" Barry said turning to face her.

"You're open?" she asked.

"Of course I'm open my dear. I've served this community for over thirty years and I'll be damned if I'm going to let a zombie apocalypse stop me now. End of the world or not, people always need air freshener, especially now the dead are stinking up the place. I should do a deal actually. Buy one can of air freshener and get a second half price. I'll make a bloody killing," Barry said as he hurriedly made a special offer sign and hung it from the air freshener section on the shelving unit.

"I'm looking for my boyfriend, Rod Hay? His bike is outside and he was wearing his cycling gear. Have you seen him?" She asked.

Barry paused for a second, sucking the end of his pen as he recalled the events of the day before.

"Ah you must be Mel! He was in here yesterday. Nice fella but a bit harassed as he had just fought off the advances of a tubby naked old woman zombie and a one armed transvestite zombie. I tried to get him to stay but he was adamant he wanted to get home to you. He took a vehicle from outside. Hasn't made it back then eh?" he said.

She shook her head and looked to the floor to hide her upset.

"Are you going to try and find him?" Barry asked.

"I have to," she replied.

"I understand. And I suppose just like your fella there's no talking you into staying here with me, just till things calm down out there?" He asked.

His question was met with a determined shake of the head.

"I didn't think so. You have the same look in your eye that he had. Here..." he said, throwing her a bottle of water, "Drink this and stay off that rum I can see poking out of your fancy belt. You need to be thinking straight if you're going to find him." He added.

"Thanks," she replied, catching the bottle and opening the door to leave, "You know you really should close the shop?"

"So every bugger keeps telling me!" Barry responded with a smile. "Good luck out there and if you need anything, anything at all, I'm open 6am to 7.30pm daily but I close at 12pm on a Sunday. Everyone's welcome unless you're dead then you'll get a clout around the head with this!" he continued, swooshing his axe handle through the air.

She left BJ & J Owens, dislodged Rod's bike from the rear wheel of the Mini Cooper and pulled away, stalling at the mouth of Balfour Street as it opened up onto Greenway Road.

"He could be anywhere," she said to herself, trying to decide which direction to take.

Right could take her to Weston Point but why would Rod take a route that would send him further away from his home? Left could take her directly towards Runcorn Old Town or it could take her to Heath Road, past the Medical Centre then back to the Old Town.

"The medical centre!" she said.

What if he had been injured? If so, it would be the logical place for him to go. It was only a short drive away and now she had the idea in her mind that he might be there, she couldn't ignore it.

The journey to Heath Road Medical Centre was similar to what she had already seen of her town. Houses were abandoned or boarded up. People lay dead in driveways, surrounded by their belongings whilst zombies fed on their remains. Was there anywhere in Runcorn that hadn't fallen to the zombie outbreak? She didn't think so and the more she saw of her town the more hope that Rod was OK left her heart.

She arrived at the medical centre, parking the Mini next to a Ford Mondeo Estate. She looked into the Mondeo's interior. Droplets of dried blood were present on the gear stick and steering wheel. With her heart beating out of her chest, she took a deep breath and walked towards the open doorway, the smell of death becoming stronger with each step.

In the waiting room the cause of the stench became apparent. Three dead zombies lay over chairs. Behind the Perspex window of the reception area were another two zombies. Receptionists, identifiable only by their uniforms such was the extent of the damage inflicted to their faces. She looked beyond the waiting room to the small corridor which had several closed doors on either side. At the end of the corridor was a door marked 'Staff Only' that stood half open, a bloodied hand print smeared across its middle. The sound of her heart beating was deafening and her legs felt like jelly as she approached and pushed the door open.

In front of her was a man knelt down, facing away from her, sobbing over the body of a dead male. The body was mostly obscured by the man but what she could see was a leg and it was covered with cycle leg warmers and bib shorts. She knew instantly it was Rod and dropped the Bat'leth in shock, the noise causing the man to turn.

"Mel? Is that you?"

The man was Darren Hay, Rod's brother. She couldn't believe what she was seeing. After convincing herself that he would be OK she was not prepared for this and Darren's presence added to her distress. With vision blurring, she suddenly felt hot and disorientated. The room closed in and her chest tightened. Feeling trapped and restricted by her attire, she removed her Hulk fist, cape, utility belt and the Teenage Mutant Ninja Turtle Mask covering her eyes then slumped to the ground and sat in silence, staring at her boyfriend's corpse.

"I've been trying to find you both. I went to your home this morning but you weren't there. The door was open and there were dead zombies everywhere. I thought maybe you were attacked but got away. The only thing I could think of was to try every medical centre in town starting with the nearest first. That's how I found him," Darren cried.

Mel could not find the words to respond and instead sat trance like, gazing at the bloodied mess that was once Rod's face.

"I've been trying to make sense of what happened. Someone did this to him but why? Over medical supplies? They killed him over medical supplies? Who would do such a thing?" he continued.

"It wasn't medical supplies. He was infected, look at his arm. He was already a zombie when they did this to him, it was self-defence," she said finding her voice.

Darren looked his brother over, noticing the wound on his arm for the first time. He broke down, placing his head into Rod's cold dead chest. He was inconsolable. The pain, loneliness and fear his brother must have endured played through his mind. The more he thought about it the harder he cried. Mel on the other hand said nothing; her body was numb from what she had found.

For the longest time they just sat there. Darren expressing deep despair and Mel, well, she was struggling to feel anything at all. Eventually Darren became exhausted and could cry no longer.

Silence fell and with just her thoughts, Mel finally began to feel something. She felt anger and hate. Anger towards the world and hate towards the zombies responsible for taking Rod away from her. She wanted vengeance for his death and desired nothing more than to set the world alight and watch it burn. She jumped to her feet and replaced the utility belt then cape before placing her hand back inside the Hulk fist and taking the mask in her hand.

"What are you doing Mel, are you leaving? You can come with me back to our place. Everyone is there. They will be so happy if you came back. Please Mel, don't leave me," Darren pleaded.

Mel stopped short of leaving the room with her back to Darren. She looked at the mask she held in her hand and thought about his words. Without Rod, she could not go back with his brother. She was happy everyone was safe, truly she was. But leaving with Darren, to be surrounded by Rod's family, would be a constant reminder of what she had lost. She wasn't ready for that, not yet. All she wanted was to be alone and to make the undead pay for what they did.

"You should go back to your family Darren," she said.

"You're not coming with me?" Darren asked, confused that she would even consider otherwise.

"Here, take this," she said, rolling her Braveheart sword along the floor towards him, "It was Rod's, it will keep you safe. Tell everyone I love them."

"Mel?" he said, the tone of his voice pleading with her not to leave.

"My name isn't Mel anymore," she replied, placing her mask back over her eyes, reclaiming the Bat'leth and leaving the room.

"I am Apocalypse Girl."

Journal Entry 10

"For the last time, what are you listening to?" I again asked 80s Dave, who had done nothing but pace back and forth while smoking cigarettes and humming along to music pumping through his headphones.

My brother had told Dave to wait for him in the spare room whilst he got ready for the ciggy run they were both going on. That was almost an hour ago and Dave was running out of patience.

"Can you even hear me over whatever that God awful noise coming out of your headphones is supposed to be? It sounds like a cat being strangled. When was the last time you took those things off your head anyway? I swear I can see skin from your ears growing over them. They'll be a part of you soon and you'll form a symbiotic relationship with your thirty year old Sony Walkman. You won't even need to press play. One twitch of your eye and the Greatest Hits of Bronski Beat will boom into your ears," I continued.

"I can hear every word you know, I'm just choosing to ignore you because I know it winds you up. I've got to get my kicks where I can these days Ace. Although, I do like your idea of me and my headphones becoming one. That would be fucking sweet kidda," Dave replied.

"So come on, put me out of my misery and hit me with it, what are you listening to?" I asked.

"Public Image Ltd lar, fucking awesome. John Lydon at his creative best. Some people say he could never top the impact of the Sex Pistols. But PIL was Johnny Rotten showing his genius. Post Punk at its most awesome kidda, pure 80s Gold. Your bro has got an awesome vintage Hitachi hi-fi with a double tape deck in his room. It works too. I banged out 'The Lunatics have Taken Over the Asylum' by Fun Boy Three earlier and it sounded fucking immense. Also very apt given our current situation. Runcorn being the asylum and the zombies being the lunatics. Anyway, I'm sure you get the comparison. You're not as stupid as you look never mind what Butty says. Where was I? Oh yeah, Public Image Ltd. I'll pick up a blank cassette tape whilst I'm out and do you a copy if you want?" he replied.

"Dave, you do know what year it is don't you? You can't just pop out to the shops for a blank cassette tape. People don't use them anymore," I explained.

"Yeah well, people are dicks," Dave said, lighting a cigarette and returning to pacing the room. "Where the hell is your brother? It's been nearly an hour lar. We could have gone and been back by now."

My brother's ears must have been burning because right on cue he opened the door and entered the room. I didn't recognise him at first due to the home made full body armour he was wearing. Butty's survivalist skills never cease to amaze me and his zombie proof suit left my jaw hanging.

Butty stood in the now open doorway, light from the corridor behind him casting a long intimidating shadow. He was wearing large leather boots which covered his ankles. Protecting the boots, he had attached several metal plates. On his legs he wore the tightest jeans I have ever seen and they left very little to the imagination. Over his knees he wore skateboarding pads and, around his waist, a tool belt which held several knives of various sizes, a crowbar, sling shot and a bag of marbles. Over his stomach and chest he wore a stab proof vest. Covering his elbows he had more skateboarding pads. Protecting his lower arms, he wore shin pads and over his upper arms were plastic tubing. On his head was a builder's hard hat but even with all of that, the thing I could not avert my eyes from was the lamp shade around his neck.

"Do you remember when we were kids and me, you and Paul Williams used to make our own costumes and pretend we were Transformers? Well that's what you look like now. Optimus Shite; Halfwit in Disguise," I teased. "Go on then let's hear it, explain yourself."

"There's nothing to explain. What you're looking at here is the perfect zombie protection suit." Butty replied.

"I wouldn't really call it a suit. More of a mixed bag of random crap you've found lying about the house," I said, trying to hold back the laughter.

"Crap? You have a lot to learn little brother. You see these boots? Big and heavy and almost impossible to damage. There's not a zombie roaming the Earth that could chomp through these bad boys and just to make sure, I've covered them in metal plates. Not only extra protection but great for causing damage should I have to boot any of the bastards," Butty explained.

"They look heavy, you'll struggle to kick a pebble in those never mind a zombie," I said.

"If it were you wearing them then maybe, but me? Piece of cake. I've been doing squats in preparation John, don't you worry," my brother replied.

"Squats? In those jeans? I'm surprised you can walk never mind bend down. They do look familiar though, have I seen them before?" I asked, intrigued.

"You have, I've stolen them from Jonathon. You see, whilst you guys were taking the piss out him for wearing skinny jeans, it got me thinking. Tight jeans are perfect anti zombie trousers. Think about it. The last thing you want to be wearing when being chased down by the living dead is baggy clothing. Tight clothing is a must. Nothing for them to grab hold of you see? In fact, I reckon the next chance we get, we pick up skinny jeans for everyone," Butty said.

"Fuck that lar. I'd rather take my chances than squeeze into those things. No offence but you look like you only need to sneeze and you'll be sliced in three. I can even tell what side you get dressed. It can't be comfortable? Your junk looks like a squashed bull frog! It's almost putting me off my smokes!" Dave interjected.

"Just a minute, did you just say they're Jonathon's jeans? How did you manage to take them without him knowing?" I asked.

"Easy. He was fast asleep snuggling up to our Emily and his jeans were draped over the back of a chair. I just took them," Butty replied.

It's difficult to explain the rage that built up inside of me on hearing that my daughter was snuggling up to her boyfriend minus his jeans and, if this was a cartoon, my face would have been deep red and steam would have been blowing out of my ears! Then as quickly as the anger came it disappeared again. I can no longer treat my daughter as a child. I must treat her as an adult and trust her to make the right decisions. If this would have happened a few days earlier, before the zombies had arrived, then the outcome would have been very different. Still, I was glad Jonathon wasn't in the room. If he was I don't believe I would have been capable of anything resembling rational thought.

"The stab vest I can understand as it's not just zombies we have to watch out for but what's with the lampshade? You look like a dog after an operation with that thing around your neck. Have you got some stitches you are trying not to nibble?" Dave teased.

"You can mock, but nothing is biting my neck with this thing protecting it that's for sure. Right then, I'm ready to go, Get your gear on and we'll be off," Butty said to Dave.

"What do you mean get my gear on? I'm ready now," Dave replied.

"You can't seriously be considering going out dressed like that? You have no protection. What will you do if you find yourself surrounded by zombies? Use your fists?" Butty responded, becoming agitated.

"If it came down to it yeah I would but I won't have to, not with this bad boy. Throw me the Battle Paddle John," Dave instructed.

I threw the Battle Paddle to Dave who began swinging and swooping it around the room as if to prove to Butty how effective it was and he was right. It may not be the most elegant of zombie slaying weapons but without it, both Dave and I may not have escaped the mayonnaise factory with our lives. Butty wasn't impressed however and scoffed at Dave's paddle swooping.

"Yes I've looked over your 'Battle Paddle' Dave. Clumsy and impractical if you ask me. I'm astounded you've lasted this long with that lump of plastic for protection," Butty said.

"This lump of plastic saved both mine and your brother's lives. Where I go, it goes. No compromise," Dave replied defiantly.

Whilst Butty tried and failed to convince 80s Dave that he needed more protection than just a large plastic mayonnaise (yuck!) stirring instrument, I heard footsteps out on the hall and the voices of teenagers whispering. It was Emily and Jonathon and just as I was about to rush to the door and confront my daughter's boyfriend for snuggling up to her minus his pants (the anger didn't disappear for long) Dave pressed the Battle Paddle into my chest, restricting my movement.

"Don't be hasty kidder, all you will do is upset Emily and you don't need that John, not with all the other shit going on around here. Have a quiet word with the randy little sod when it's just the two of you, when nobody else is around. That'll do the trick," Dave advised.

"Wise words and good advice. Surprising really coming from a man that thinks his best defence against the undead is a giant plastic spoon," Butty interjected, shaking his head in disapproval.

"Just you wait Ace, I'll show you how effective the Battle Paddle can be, just you wait," Dave replied defiantly, lighting another cigarette and throwing a smoke to my brother who gladly accepted.

Then Jonathon and Emily entered the room. I quickly and without thought of consequence, grabbed the Battle Paddle from Dave whilst he was distracted with his cigarette and repeatedly smashed it into Jonathon's face. Emily screamed as my relentless attack continued and blood and teeth flew from the boy's mouth. So enraged was I with Jonathon for spending the night cuddled up to my daughter without his trousers that I couldn't stop my attack and it took both Dave and Butty to pull me away from him. By this point though it was too late and Jonathon was dead.

Or that's what played out in my head when I laid eyes on the little shit. If it wasn't for Dave's out of character words of wisdom my rage fuelled daydream could have become a reality. It's a good job I had heeded Dave's words because Jonathon entered the room wearing cargo pants, my brother's cargo pants to be exact.

"Morning all. Hey Dad, what do you think of Uncle Butty's anti zombie armour? Pretty cool isn't it? I helped him design it. Wearing Jonathon's skinny jeans was my idea. I figured that if we don't wear loose clothing it gives the zombies less to grab. Jonathon agreed to let Uncle Butty use them for the ciggy run in exchange for a pair of cargo pants. Next chance we get, I think we need to get some tight jeans, maybe even leggings," Emily said.

I turned to my brother who was smiling at me whilst offering a look that confirmed my suspicions. The bastard had been winding me up. Again! He hadn't taken the jeans from Jonathon whilst he was sleeping at all. Jonathon had willingly given them to him. Butty knew what my reaction would be and he was hoping to see me lose my shit and go ape on the boy. Thank god I didn't but now I was riddled with guilt following my hellish fantasy where I pummelled his face into a pulp with the Battle Paddle.

"Gutted lar, now I can't call you skinny jeans anymore. I'll just have to stick with Scrappy Do instead and if I were you I'd fill your belly with Scooby snacks now as you've got a busy morning ahead of you fortifying Diant Towers. John will show you and Emily what needs doing, as soon as the colour returns to his face that is. Come on then Butty lad let's get a move on. There's ciggies waiting to be looted and I'll be fucking pissed if we're late to the party and there's nothing left. Knowing my luck the only brand remaining will be Silk Cut. Honestly, why anyone who smokes would choose Silk fucking Cut as their brand beggars belief. You might as well walk around sucking air. Actually you'd probably get a better toke sucking the toxic polluted air around here than you would from pulling on one of those lame arse tabs. The type of people that smoke Silk Cut are the type of people that smoke because they think it makes them look cool. Scene smokers that don't know the meaning of the word dedication. Not like me Ace, I'm in it for the long haul. Right then, I'll go start up the Thunderbird," Dave said, finishing his rant and leaving the room.

"He really takes his smoking seriously doesn't he?" Butty asked me, to which I nodded in response, "Emily look after your Dad for me, we'll be back soon I promise."

Butty hugged Emily before slowly walking out of the room like a robotic John Wayne. In all honestly, I held a real concern that this was going to be the last time I would see Dave and my brother but nothing I could say would stop them from making their little shopping trip. Captain Cocksure and Sir Smokes-a-Lot would not have even considered it as a possibility but the reality was they were taking a trip into the unknown. I hoped to God they knew what they were doing.

Irregular Urban Survivors

Tony began to gasp, his parched throat jolting him into consciousness. Struggling to swallow, he desperately attempted to lubricate his throat with saliva. A task that was proving increasingly difficult to do as the cold winter air filled his mouth. Lifting his head from the drop down tray, he opened his eyes to see blue sky through the broken carbon fibre and metal frame of the Boeing 737, the cool morning air responsible for his dehydration.

He quickly lowered his head, averting his eyes from the bright blue sky. Having been unconscious for almost twenty four hours, he struggled to focus and chose to concentrate his gaze on the floor of the aeroplane.

With vision steadying, he noticed a small bottle of orange juice resting against his right foot. Reaching down he grabbed at the bottle of juice, desperate to quench his thirst and coat his throat in much needed fluid. In his haste he lunged forward with speed but his seatbelt was fastened tight, forcing the strap to dig deep into his waist. The pain made his right leg jolt and he watched as the orange juice, now free from his foot, rolled along the floor before finally resting in the palm of a cold pale blue hand which reached out from underneath the seat in front.

Tony knew who the hand belonged to. He recognised the Rolex wrapped around its wrist. The watch was a fake of course and he knew it to be so. Reality TV stars do not earn enough to afford an original Rolex Oyster Perpetual Datejust. The pale frozen hand belonged to Michael Wood or 'Mikey' as he was known to fans of the new hit reality show 'Famous for 15 Minutes', where contestants try to outdo each other with acts of extreme stupidity to win votes from the public and a cash prize of £25,000. Mikey had won the show by bathing naked in a bath filled with live eels whilst singing 'When Will I Be Famous' by Bros repeatedly for twelve hours. Tony was aware of the show as it was difficult to escape the constant barrage of television, radio, magazine and social media buzz surrounding the series. Every time he turned on his television, listened to his radio or logged on to Twitter and Facebook, everyone would be talking about the 'Wild and Crazy' antics the contestants were prepared to do to win the show, the money and the fame that came with it. Tony, unlike a large proportion of the British population, had never subjected himself to viewing it. Big Brother, Tool Academy, The Bachelor, Famous for 15 Minutes.. They were all the same to him and they served the same purpose - to dumb down the British population, acting as nothing more than a distraction from the economic and social unrest that had engulfed the country in recent years.

Tony had been quite proud that he didn't know the names of any of the 'Famous for 15 Minutes' contestants or indeed what they looked like. That however, had all changed a day earlier at Liverpool's John Lennon Airport, when Mikey had made his presence known to everyone with his appalling behaviour. He had screamed at the attendants in the departure lounge for not allowing him to fast track his way onto the flight before everyone else. Rants of "Don't you know who I am?" and "I'm Michael 'Mikey' Wood, winner of 'Famous for 15 minutes', I'll have you fired for this!" had echoed through the departure lounge. His arrogant diva like behaviour continued on the plane where his demands to be moved to a better seat with more leg room had fallen on deaf ears with the air stewards. Obviously this 'celebrity' had never flown with a budget airline before.

Tony was familiar with this type of behaviour. As the frontman with British rockers Terrorvision and Laika Dog, Tony Wright had been confronted with more than his fair share of wannabes over the years. Back in the mid-1990s, Tony was a regular on TV music panel show 'Never Mind the Buzzcocks' and would often find himself in the company of so called celebrities, full of deluded self-importance and inexcusable rudeness. It was to his annoyance that he still found himself surrounded by these people and had often thought it must be something about him, something that attracts the talentless and fame hungry. Though he had often wished it, this was the first time that one of them had actually died on him.

Tony unclipped his seatbelt and reached to the floor, taking the bottle of orange juice that was resting in the hand of the dead reality TV star. Drinking greedily, he lined his throat with the cold, thirst quenching liquid. It felt good and for the first time since waking, he found his voice.

"What the fuck happened here?"

He pushed himself out of his seat and rose to his feet. Assessing the damage, he thought it nothing short of a miracle he was unharmed. The scene was gruesome, with mangled bodies, trays of airline meals, hand luggage and dispensed oxygen masks littering the fractured passenger cabin. He quickly began to shiver, as if his body had all of a sudden realised how cold and exposed it was. Looking for something to keep warm, he noticed a leopard print fake fur coat underneath the body of a dead air stewardess. She was a mess. Lying face down in the aisle, her left foot had twisted an almost full 180 degree turn and her right leg, having been sliced from foot to thigh, was opened up like a freshly gutted fish.

Tony tugged at the leopard print fake fur coat, pulling it from underneath the stewardess and in the process flipping her over onto her front. He recognised her as the stewardess that, on take-off, had had the unfortunate job of handling the difficult and petulant Michael 'Mikey' Wood and did so with a degree of expertise too. After several demands to be moved to another seat, the stewardess had been stern and strong when dealing with Mikey and she had done so repeatedly. That is until a rather loud and public tantrum from the reality TV star had forced her to lose her cool and threaten to remove his fake Rolex and shove it so far up his arse that he'd need a rectal exam whenever he wanted to know the time. A threat that was met with a round of applause from the passengers and that was finally enough to shut him up.

Like everyone else, Tony had overheard the angry exchange and admired her greatly for standing up to the wannabe celebrity. Now he was looking down at her bloodied and bruised lifeless face. He looked to the name badge pinned to her blazer. The name read Sarah Layton. He needed to get off the plane.

Tony walked down the aisle towards the front of the plane. He pulled hard on the passenger door handle but it would not open. The crash had damaged the door's inflatable seal used to lock in cabin pressure. A team of World's Strongest Man contestants would not be able to open it with the seal still in place.

"Help me."

Tony turned his attention from the door and looked back along the aisle to see where the plea for help had come from.

"Help me, please."

He looked to the centre left of the aeroplane where a heap of deceased passengers lay piled up on top of each other in the seating area directly over the wing. He quickly walked along the aisle and examined the bodies. At the very bottom, between a disfigured arm and a torn foot, was a heavily bruised mouth and it spoke to him.

"Don't leave me please."

He began to quickly remove body from body, lowering the deathly mound and reducing the pressure of weight on the man at the bottom. Finally free, the man shakily rose to his feet, revealing his heavily bruised and bloodied face. Tony found a small carton of water at his feet, peeled back the silver foiled lid and poured it into the man's mouth.

"Thank you," the man said gratefully as the cool liquid lubricated his dry throat.

"Are you ok? I thought I was the only one alive on this plane. My name's Tony," he asked.

"I'm Mike, Mike Green. Man it hurts to talk," Mike said, wincing in pain when touching his face.

"Well you've suffered severe bruising to your face, I'm surprised you can talk at all," Tony said.

"Thanks for pulling me out of there. I thought I was going to die with those people on top of me. What do you think happened? Do you remember anything about the crash?" Mike asked.

"I have no idea what happened. The last thing I remember is taking off from Liverpool, some dick sat in front of me mouthing off demanding to be moved seats, the stewardess putting him in his place and then nothing. I don't remember a thing after that. I must have blacked out and I came around a few minutes ago. What about you, do you remember anything?" Tony asked.

"Well, I remember the take-off the same as you and I remember the man complaining. I'd seen him on TV making a tit out of himself a few weeks back. I suppose he thought he was some kind of big shot screaming to be moved seats. Probably thought with the plane being nearly empty he could sit wherever he wanted. To be honest, I've seen people sit wherever they want on these budget airlines before, it happens all the time but I guess he yelled at the wrong stewardess. Then I remember looking out of the window, hoping to see my house as we flew over it when the plane suddenly dropped in altitude and oxygen masks came down. People screamed and something seemed to be happening down at the front of the plane. What it was I don't know but I saw one of the air stewards covered in blood and passengers began to leave their seats, heading towards the back in a panic. Then that was it. I first woke a few hours ago and I have been drifting in and out of sleep until I opened my eyes to see you pulling on the door over there. Lucky for me I woke when I did eh?" Mike said.

"The door at the front of the plane is sealed shut. We can try this one over the wing and then the one at the back if need be. One of them has got to work and then we can get out of here and see where the hell we are," Tony replied whilst peeking through a small frost coated window but all he could see was the wing and the grey of the road beneath the wreckage of the aircraft.

Tony and Mike tried both doors but like the first, they too were sealed shut. The only exit available was the through the torn roof above Tony's seat. Tony climbed up onto the seat and lifted himself out of the passenger hold. On top of the plane, a harsh cold breeze brushed against his face and he felt thankful for the leopard print fake fur jacket he was wearing.

"What do you see?" Mike shouted from inside the passenger hold.

Tony looked directly ahead to the cockpit. The nose of the plane had pushed against a large wall. Beyond the wall, was a high rise block of flats. He looked to his right to see that although still attached, the wing had become damaged and unstable and the engine that was once connected was now missing. Any applied weight could certainly separate it from the body of the airplane. He turned and looked to the left wing. Thankfully, it appeared to be largely unaffected and would be the perfect way to climb down to the road below, which was littered with suitcases spilled from the damaged cargo hold. Also on the road, lay the corpses of passengers, their contorted carcasses resting in frozen pools of rich glistening blood.

A deafening creaking sound filled the air, quickly followed by a heavy splash. Tony turned to see the cause of the noise. Behind him was a canal and, beyond that, a river. In the river lay one half of a large through arch bridge. It was a hanging support frame that had broken free from the intact half of the bridge and fallen into the river.

"Tony, what do you see?" Mike asked once again.

Tony hurried back to the hole he'd climbed through and helped Mike to lift himself out of the passenger hold, joining him on top of the plane.

"See for yourself," he said, witnessing Mike absorb the apocalyptic landscape in which they found themselves.

Mike looked at the corpses and suitcases on the road, then shifted his attention to the river and destroyed bridge. To Tony's surprise Mike began to laugh uncontrollably.

"Ha-ha holy shit! Do you know where we are? This is Runcorn man, my home town. That there is the River Mersey and that's the Runcorn Bridge or what used to be the Runcorn Bridge. Fuck me, we've crashed in my home town! We're on Mersey Road! I said didn't I, the last thing I remember is looking out of the window hoping to see my house as we flew over. Well there it fucking is, over the wall next to Churchill Mansions," Mike said, pointing to his house. "That's where we've got to go. I've got clothes and food and we can get cleaned up, call the police and figure out what's going on."

"That's what I don't understand, the police, why haven't the emergency services turned up? I mean look around. A plane crash, a destroyed bridge and bodies everywhere… why has nobody come to help?" Tony asked.

"I don't know. Nothing's making much sense at the moment. Let's just get down from here and head to my place, we'll be out of the cold at least," Mike suggested.

Tony slid from the top of the plane onto the left wing then helped Mike down to join him. They walked along the wing to where the edge was touching the road and then carefully jumped down.

Mike slowly walked out amongst the scattered luggage and bodies. Looking over the corpses, something wasn't adding up. The ravished skin, ripped open flesh and muscle torn bodies of the dead did not match the scene of the crash. He cast his mind back to the bodies inside the aircraft that he had been trapped beneath. Yes they were dead, with broken and bloodied limbs but none of them looked like this. There was something more going on here.

Tony was inspecting the aeroplane and, in particular, the nose of the craft which rested against the large wall. He was brushing his hand against the cool exterior of the plane as he walked towards the cockpit when his foot pushed into something hard. He looked down to see his foot had kicked into the stomach of a frozen body which had been crushed by the underbelly of the cockpit. Poking out lay a heavily tattooed arm with the hand holding a wooden walking stick. He looked to Mike, who was bent over a passenger inspecting the injuries they had sustained.

"You ok over there?" he asked.

"This doesn't make sense. This man has had his stomach ripped open and his intestines are missing. Missing! He's not the only one either. All of these people look like they have been pulled, torn and ripped apart. Someone or something did this to them post-accident," Mike replied.

Quack!

"Did you here that?" Mike asked.

Quack, quack!

They both looked to the embankment leading down towards the Manchester Ship Canal and the River Mersey. Waddling into view appeared a lone duck with blood stained feathers. The duck stalled when it reached the edge of Mersey Road and appeared to stare at Mike who stared back, more in bewilderment at the sight of the gore stained bird than anything else. The duck started to waddle from side to side manically, quacking and croaking over and over again. He looked down to the body at his feet then looked back to the duck. As quickly as the thought entered his head he dismissed it. How could a duck or ducks do this to a human? It simply couldn't be possible. Then the duck attacked and in an instant he knew he was right. He grabbed a nearby suitcase and thwarted the devilish bird's advances by bashing it over and over again until it resembled repeatedly hit road kill.

"Are you thinking what I'm thinking?" Mike asked Tony.

Mike realised that Tony wasn't looking at him but looking past him to the canal embankment. The noise of ducks and geese quacking, squawking and waddling filled the air and he turned his head to see over twenty blood coated birds heading towards him. He tried to run away but his injuries made this difficult and the ducks and geese quickly gained on him.

"Run! Head to my house!" Mike shouted to Tony.

Further along the wall were steps leading up to a small housing estate next to Churchill Mansions. Tony could make it but he had doubts about his companion and wasn't about to leave him. He reached down and yanked the wooden walking stick from the dead man's hand. Without thought for his own safety, he ran past Mike and began swinging wildly at the oncoming ducks and geese. Feathers and blood filled the air as one by one they fell. Both he and Mike had been amazingly fortunate to survive the crash and he was damned if a bunch of rabid birds were to be the death of them after everything they had been through.

After several frenzied minutes he was done or at least he thought he was. A small duck had made it past and was nipping at Mike's ankles.

"Use this!" Tony shouted, throwing the walking stick to Mike who used it to bring an end to the infected devil duck.

He defended himself so forcefully that the walking stick broke under the ferocity of the hits and lay in splintered pieces next to the destroyed demon duck.

"Fuck you, you shit!" Mike yelled at the battered remains of his attacker.

"Are you ok, Mike? Are you hurt?" Tony asked with concern.

"No more that I already was. Just a few scratches on my ankles, that's all. Come on, let's get off the streets before more of those little bastards arrive, follow me," he replied.

They walked away from Mersey Road, up the steps towards Churchill Mansions and Mike's house where they were greeted by an assortment of human remains with various injuries but they all shared one similarity. They had been thrown from a great height and lay splattered across the ground, their insides sprayed across the cold concrete floor.

"Are these passengers too?" Mike asked.

"I don't think so; these folk have been dead for a while. They either jumped from this here block of flats or they were pushed. A plane crash couldn't have done this, they're too far away from the accident plus that one over there has been decapitated. Something else is responsible for this. There's a lot more going on here than we know. We best get off the streets," Tony replied.

Mike opened the door to his house and they walked inside, Tony entering the large rectangular living room and Mike hobbling into the kitchen. In the living room a 50 inch flat screen television was positioned next to a tall standalone lamp, both in front of a large window overlooking Mersey Road and the plane crash they had escaped. Pointed at the television were two leather reclining chairs and a large leather sofa rested against the wall separating the room from the kitchen.

Tony walked to the window and looked out, studying the apocalyptic view.

"I've tried phoning the emergency services but the line is dead," Mike said entering the living room whilst limping notably. "Heating is on. It's freezing in here don't you think? You could try the TV, see if there is anything on the news," he groaned, sitting on his sofa, gripping both his ankles tightly.

"You ain't looking too good? Did that duck do more damage than you first thought?" Tony asked.

"I'm fine, really," Mike replied through gritted teeth, the tone of his voice telling a different story to the words spoken.

Tony picked up a framed photograph from the window sill. The picture was of a male and female holding each other in a loving embrace.

"Do you live here alone?" Tony asked.

"No, I rent this place with a friend of mine. His name is Gary Littlemore. That's him in the picture you're holding and the girl is his fiancée, Sharon Grimshaw. He's probably at her place," replied Mike, sweat now dripping freely from his forehead.

A loud clanging noise, like something heavy being knocked to the floor, came from the room directly above.

"What's up there?" Tony asked of Mike whilst looking to the ceiling.

"Gary's bedroom, he must be home after all," Mike replied as he struggled to his feet and hobbled out to the bottom of the stairway. "Gary mate, it's Mike, you OK up there? Come down man, you won't believe what's happened."

Heavy footsteps were heard walking along the hallway towards the top of the stairway. They were so heavy that Tony watched as the woven wicker shade that covered the living room light fitting swung from side to side.

"You see anything?" he asked of Mike.

"Not yet but I can hear someone… OH FUCK!" Mike proclaimed as his house mate Gary came tumbling down the stairs, landing on top of him.

It took every ounce of strength to prevent Gary's gnashing teeth biting his face. Only his hands pushing against the dry flaking skin of his housemate's jawline prevented it. But there was one thing he could not avert and that was the putrid drool dripping from Gary's mouth down into his own.

Tony ran into the hallway and booted Gary hard in the side of his face. The force of the blow threw the crazed housemate from on top of Mike; his body landed twisted against the front door.

"For fuck sake Gary, what was that about?" Mike complained whilst being helped to his feet.

Gary didn't offer an explanation for his cannibalistic actions. Instead he groaned and grunted whilst jaggedly rising to his feet. Mike and Tony could not believe what they were seeing. Gary's ankle had snapped and crunched under the weight of his body, twisting further with every step he took. With the injury apparently having no effect he stumbled forward, reaching out towards his intended targets, drool slobbering from his pale skeletal mouth.

"What do you think is wrong with him?" Mike asked.

"Not sure. He looks pretty hungry to me," Tony replied.

"Gary, do you want me to rustle you up a sandwich mate?" Mike asked.

Tony and Mike walked backwards into the living room, keeping a good distance between themselves and Gary.

"I think he might want something more substantial than a sandwich," Mike added.

"Yeah, like you or me by the looks of things. Well he can fuck right off!" Tony pronounced.

He quickly marched to the standalone lamp, removed the shade and flicked the switch to light the bulb. With his plan being to electrocute Gary, he ran towards him using the lamp as a spear. What he hadn't accounted for was the length of the electrical wire and when only inches away from his target the wire became taut and the plug sprung from the wall socket, removing all power. He looked down at the electricity void lamp in despair then back to Gary as the bulb smashed against his stomach, exposing the small bayonet capped tip of the lamp which then penetrated the skin and slithered through his body with ease.

Still Gary pushed forward, being speared by the lamp through his abdomen did nothing to slow him down. He edged forward some more, sliding further down the thin pole and closer to Tony who stood motionless in disbelief, the lamp still in his hands.

"Fuck this!" Tony said.

Grabbing Gary by the trouser belt and neck line of his shirt, Tony pulled him free from the lamp pole and launched him through the large window overlooking Mersey Road. Mike joined him at the window and they both looked to the twitching body on the road below.

"Sorry about the window. The lamp too. I hope you've got house insurance?" Tony asked apologetically.

"I have but I don't think the policy covers me for breakages due to cannibalistic attacks from housemates!" came Mike's reply.

Mike hobbled to his couch and collapsed heavily on the soft leather cushions. He was exhausted and could feel the start of a fever burn through him. All he wanted was to sleep and sleep he did, solidly for just over an hour.

Whilst Mike rested, Tony spent his time securing the broken window the best he could by moving wardrobes from the bedrooms upstairs and placing them against the opening.

Exhausted, he pushed the last wardrobe against the window and, wiping the sweat from his forehead, looked one last time to the road outside. There he saw Mike's housemate, who after enduring being speared by a lamp and thrown through a window, was staring back at him with rancid drool dripping from his pale lips.

"How the hell are you still alive?" Tony said, completely perplexed at what he was witnessing.

He had seen enough and positioned the final wardrobe against the window then took a seat facing Mike and concern for his new companion grew. It was clear from his sweat sodden sleeping face he had not been truthful about the extent of his injuries. Be it through not wanting to worry his friend or from denial, it was evident that Mike was in pain and he thrashed back and forth feverishly in his sleep with sweat spilling from every pore. Rather than injuries from the crash being the cause, it appeared to be stemming from his lower legs, where the rabid duck had been pecking away earlier. He needed to be watched. If his health was to deteriorate even more, then medical attention would be required and from what Tony had seen of Runcorn so far, he wasn't sure that was going to be an option.

Mike's thrashing became so violent he woke himself from his sleep and sat up quickly in a daze, unaware of his surroundings and with panic filled eyes.

"How are you holding up, Mike?" Tony asked.

"I'm warm; don't you think it's warm? It must be like 40 degrees in here," Mike replied wearily.

"You've got a fever, I'll get something to cool you down," Tony replied.

He left the living room and entered the kitchen where he soaked a tea towel in cold water before returning.

Holding the cool wet tea towel to Mike's forehead, he looked down to his friend's legs and noticed blood had soaked through his socks, dripping onto his trainers and the floor below his feet.

"When Gary comes back, tell him that you're sorry and you didn't mean to throw him through the window or stab him with the lamp. He's a good guy he'll under... he'll understand," Mike muttered groggily before falling back into a fevered sleep.

Tony took the opportunity to inspect Mike's ankle by removing the trainer from his right foot and pulling down his blood soaked sock. It was not a pleasant sight. Several open lesions covered his leg from the heel all the way up to his shin, leaking out rich sticky plasma. Between the open sores, lived dark veins, tracking up the leg towards his thigh. This confirmed his suspicion that the cause of Mike's fever was not through the injuries sustained from the plane crash but from the duck attack.

He rushed back into the kitchen area and frantically opened cupboards and drawers looking for a first aid pack or anything that he could use to treat the injuries. There was nothing and instead he soaked tea towel after tea towel in hot water. On his return, it took him by surprise to see Mike was no longer passed out on the sofa but instead standing at the window, his back turned from Tony.

"Mike? Come and sit yourself back down and let me look at those legs of yours. It's not a good idea for you to be up and about. Not until we've calmed that fever down at least," he said.

Mike did not respond. Instead he stayed motionless looking out of the window. Tony's gut told him that something was wrong; he was only hoping it wasn't what he thought it was. Slowly he approached until close enough to hear Mike's laboured and hoarse breathing. Reaching forward to place a hand on Mike's shoulder he spoke his name. Mike turned to face him, revealing his gaunt pale face, stark white eyes and twitching nose which was busy sniffing the air between them. Tony quickly retracted his hand and retreated, stumbling backwards and tripping over the lamp he had used to spear Gary. Without hesitation he grabbed the lamp and jumped to his feet.

"Sorry pal!" Tony said apologetically.

He charged at Mike, spearing him through his stomach with the lamp sending him crashing through the wardrobes, out of the window and down to the road outside.

Cautiously Tony stepped up to the broken window and looked through. It hadn't taken long for Mike to stagger back to his feet and, with the lamp still speared through his stomach, he shuffled towards the house. He wasn't alone either. Several crazed ducks and geese had joined him and more were waddling over from the embankment separating the road from the Manchester Ship Canal. Also with him, pulling its decaying corpse towards the house, was the twisted body of his housemate.

"The only way to kill a zombie is to destroy the brain, nothing else works," said the voice of the man stood behind him.

Tony quickly grabbing the first thing he could find to defend himself and turned to face the man.

"What are you going to do with that, place it under my head and sing me a lullaby? My name's Nick, Nick Fieldsend. Don't worry fella I mean you no harm," Nick said, introducing himself to a cushion wielding Tony.

"How did you get in?" Tony asked defensively whilst keeping a tight grip of the cushion.

"You left the front door unlocked. Zombies might be flummoxed by door handles but people aren't. You've got a lot to learn my friend," Nick said with a smile.

"Twice. You've said the word zombies twice now. Is that what you think this is?" Tony asked.

Nick laughed uncontrollably, so much so that his ribs began to ache. After several very loud and over the top belly laughs he wiped the tears away from his eyes and composed himself.

"I'm sorry mate, I didn't mean to laugh like that. Forgive me, really I'm sorry. I lost myself for a minute there. It's probably a combination of all the booze I've been drinking and the amount of dead bastards I've had to kill. What do you remember from yesterday?" he asked.

"Nothing really, not till I woke this morning in that plane wreck out there and everyone was dead," he replied.

"Let me fill you in. Yesterday the world went to shit and almost everyone turned into zombies. Those that didn't were either eaten by zombies, became infected by zombies and then turned into zombies or, like the two of us, are fighting to survive against zombies. Bloody hell, I said zombies quite a lot then, I'll have to come up with a new name for them. How about... dead fucks? What do you say Tony?" Nick said.

"How the hell do you know my name?" a puzzled Tony asked.

"Well I've got every Terrorvision album and I've watched you live six times so I should bloody know your name. I thought it was you when I saw you climb out of the plane. I would have popped down to help but the last time I tried to help someone it didn't end so well. In fact, you yanked a walking stick from his frozen dead hand earlier. But then I thought fuck it what if it is you and I don't even say as much as hello? I'd never forgive myself and I'm bloody glad I did because it bloody is! Fuck me, Tony Wright as I live and breathe. Here, have a swig of this you look like you could do with it," Nick replied, offering a freshly opened bottle of Jack Daniels.

Tony gladly accepted the bottle and drank from it greedily. After everything that had happened, the warm buzz of alcohol was a welcome distraction. Following a long drink he nodded towards Nick to say thank you, handing it back to him.

"Nick was it? Nice to meet you, Nick, and cheers for the drink, I needed it," Tony said.

"There's plenty more where that came from fella. I'll take you back to my place, you'll be safe there but first I need to go shopping. I could do with a hand if you're up for it?" Nick said.

"This place of yours, it's secure?" Tony asked.

"It's only the safest place in Runcorn. Did you see the tower block outside? Well that's mine, all of it. I spent yesterday and most of last night securing the building. It was bloody tough going I can tell you but with hard work and a little help from my old friend Jack here," Nick said taking a swig from his bottle of bourbon, "Churchill Mansions is now all mine! It can be yours too if you're up for it? I don't mind sharing with Tony Wright, lead singer of Terrorvision! But as I said, we'll need to do a little shopping first."

Tony forced a smiled in reply. He was struggling to process everything that was happening. The plane crash, the devil ducks, Mike and his housemate and now Nick appearing from nowhere. It was almost too much for his tired mind to take. But his gut was telling him to trust Nick and it wasn't like he had other choices. The idea of taking a shopping trip during a zombie apocalypse wasn't exactly appealing but the promise of somewhere safe to go to when they were done was too good to turn down. Even if, as Tony was intending, it was only going to be for one night.

Following Nick's crude explanation of the zombie outbreak, the reality of the horrific world Tony found himself in sent his body into an internal panic and all he could think about was making his way home to his family. But home was over 60 miles away and if he was going to make it, he needed to formulate a plan. Before the end of the world, the journey would have taken him just over an hour by car but now its length would be impossible to determine. He needed to think things through and, at this moment in time, he had no desire to share his intentions with Nick. His gut might be saying he can trust him, but Tony's head was saying that Nick was volatile and might not react well when made aware of his intended departure.

They left Mike's house, pausing only to look at Churchill Mansions and the dead zombies that surrounded the building.

"That's your place?" Tony asked.

"Yep, I'm thinking of renaming it 'Nick's Place' or 'Fieldsend's Fortress' I'll give you the guided tour when we get back from the shops. There's a supermarket just up the road so we shouldn't be too long," Nick replied.

"What shopping do we need?" Tony asked.

"Oh, not much really. This and that. Milk and bread if we can find any fresh, more booze would be nice and oh yeah, some baby formula," Nick casually replied.

"Baby Formula?" came Tony's puzzled response.

It was a short walk from Mike's house, through Runcorn Town Centre and up to the Co-Operative Supermarket. They had encountered more 'Dead Fucks' along the way but they had mostly been pre-occupied eating the less fortunate or banging against windows and doors of buildings that housed those survivors locked away. Nick had barely given them a glance, strolling along whilst taking occasional sips from his bottle of Jack like he didn't have a care in the world. It was just as well they hadn't caught the attention of any zombies as neither had weapons. This was something Tony was all too aware of and he would willingly trade in his leopard print fake fur coat and brave the cold for a good crowbar or large knife. Nick on the other hand had arrived without a weapon and seemed in no rush to find one now.

Nick used this time to explain to Tony all he had been through since the Outbreak. How he had to kill his zombie grandmother, secure Churchill Mansions and how he witnessed rabid ducks and geese peck to death the father of a small girl and her baby sister. Then how he saved them and took them to 'Fieldsend's Fortress' and how they were the main reason for this shopping trip.

"So Sophie is the young girl and Gaby is the baby? Poor kids. It must have been horrible for them to see their father die like that. What about their mother, she must be worried about them?" Tony asked.

"Sophie had been asking about her mum and I said I'd take them home but it's not safe at the moment. You see, Sophie told me that her mum was sick and you know what that means don't you? That's right, she'll be a Dead Fuck like almost everyone else in this town. Yeah yeah I know I can't keep it from her forever but Tone, she's just a little girl and it was only yesterday she watched her Dad get eaten by what she refers to as 'duckies'. No, I can't tell her about her mum, not yet. Before you say it, yes I know there's a chance she's still alive but it's a fucking small one and I'm not prepared to risk the girls' lives by taking them home to find out. They don't need to see what it's like out here and the longer I can keep it from them the better.

They're great they are. Gaby is a little cracker and Sophie is brilliant with her. I can't wait for you to meet them but first we need supplies. Baby formula, wipes, nappies, sterilising tablets… grab as much as you can because if we don't, then someone else will. I'm just hoping I haven't left it too late and the supermarket has been looted already. We're here now anyway. Just a few more steps and…. Ah fuck!" said Nick.

Nick's expletive was not without warrant. The glass doors to the Co-Operative supermarket had been shattered and shards of glass coated the floor of the entrance. Also littering the entrance lay upturned shopping trollies, scattered tins of food and rotting fruits and breads. It was clear that it had been looted already and while Nick rushed inside, Tony took a more cautious approach, tentatively moving forward whilst checking his surroundings. He held concerns the supermarket may still harbour looters and without a weapon to defend himself he felt completely exposed. It was Nick's wailing from inside that got him moving.

Picking up a discarded tin of processed marrowfat peas and a stale loaf of bread, Tony ran inside the supermarket. What he found inside was Nick on his knees, head in his hands, moaning in front of the completely empty alcohol aisle.

"Bloody typical. The apocalypse hits and everyone in this town wants to get pissed. All the fags have gone too," Nick complained, pointing to the empty tobacco kiosk, "It's a good job I've got a large supply of booze back home or I'd be really angry."

"What about baby supplies, have you checked?" Tony asked.

"Oh there's plenty of baby stuff, it's just up that aisle next to those Dead Fucks!" Nick replied, pointing to the aisle in question.

Tony panicked, gripping the tin of peas like he was ready to throw a grenade and holding the stale bread as if it were a shield.

"Are you planning on making them a butty? I don't think they like marrowfat peas but then again who does? Anyway they've already been killed. It's the bloke that slayed them holding his neck that you should be worried about. Maybe he'd like a pea sandwich? Hey mate, fancy a pea butty?" Nick shouted.

Tony dropped the peas and bread and walked towards the aisle. On the floor lay two dead zombies, their heads battered to a pulp. Next to them was a man. His left hand was pressed against an open neck wound and in his right he held a stainless steel frying pan. Blood coated his quilted jacket and vintage Motorhead t-shirt and his long hair dripped with sweat. He was shaking, a result of the fever that burned through him.

It wasn't difficult to see what had happened and Tony knew what was coming. The fever that had taken this man was the same that had afflicted Mike. He knew it was only a matter of time before he would become what Nick called a 'Dead Fuck'.

With panic in his eyes, the man gripped the frying pan as tightly as his shaking hand would allow. This did not go unnoticed by Tony who showed the palms of his hands, gesturing that he meant him no harm.

"Easy fella, I'm not going to hurt you, I just want to help. My name is Tony and the guy over there crying about the lack of booze is Nick. Can I take a look at your neck?" he said softly.

"My name is Andy Deen, please don't leave me. My friends left me. They saw what happened and they left without as much as a goodbye. They just took what they needed and walked out. Like everything we'd been through meant nothing," Andy shivered.

"What happened, what made them leave you?" Tony asked.

"This happened," said Andy, revealing the deep pulsating wound to his neck. "It's not as bad as it looks, really. And I got those zombies good, just look at their heads man. There are pain... painkillers in here somewhere. If you could find me painkillers and something to clean and dress my neck then I'll be fine, honestly I will. Maybe I can help you guys out, what is it you're looking for? There's no more booze I can tell you that much. My friends, well, ex friends, they took it all. Cigarettes too. They filled the van, my fucking van to be exact, then scarpered. Man I loved that van. Hey if you guys help, I'll get it back and you can have it, what do you say? It's a blue 55 plate Citroen Relay. Not once has it let me down. I bought it from a guy that acquired it from another guy whose cousin stole it from a British Gas depot. Despite waxing it hundreds of times, when the sun hits it right, you can still see the British Gas logo on its side."

"We don't need a van!" Nick shouted, still glaring glumly at the looted alcohol section.

Tony knew Andy's time was almost up. He'd witnessed how quickly the fever had taken Mike and how it took no time at all for him to turn from living to living dead. He also knew that he only had two options. Option 1: Leave him to become a flesh eating monster, free to kill, to devour and deplete the dwindling living population further. Or option 2: End him now and stop his pain. To kill him so that he would not return. Option 2 would definitely be kinder but still he wrestled with the decision – a decision that was not being made any easier by Andy who was refusing to give in to his inevitable fate.

"Please, I know what you're thinking and you're wrong. Look at me, I'm fine, really. It just needs cleaning up. I'm not infected, I'm not. Look I'll show you," he pleaded, attempting to stand but failing epically.

Out of breath and removed of strength, Andy slouched against the shelving and with tears in his eyes his lips started to shiver.

"Please," he choked, the word almost inaudible such was his fear, "I don't want to die,"

Tony knelt in front of him, their faces only inches apart. He could see the tracks of the infection run from the wound on his neck, stretching out across his pale, sweat soaked face.

"I'll be straight with you Andy. The truth is you are going to die. That wound on your neck means you're infected. I can see the track marks running from it, reaching across your neck and face. That's the infection spreading. I've seen this before and it's only a matter of time before you die then come back as one of the dead fucks over there. Do you really want that to happen? You seem to be a decent guy and looking at your Motorhead t-shirt I reckon if circumstances were different we could have been pals. Now the way I see it, we have two choices. You can sit here and wait. Wait and let the pain you are feeling turn to agony as your body succumbs to the infection. It will burn through you. Your head will feel like it's going to explode. You will scream and you will beg for it to stop. Then, when your body can take no more, you will die and I will have to take that frying pan of yours and pummel your head until your brain is destroyed. Or there is choice number two…"

Tony was abruptly cut off by Nick who pressed passed him and rammed a stale French loaf into Andy's mouth, pushing through the back of his head. The assault killed him instantly.

"Bonne nuit!" said Nick in his best French accent.

"Fuck me!" Tony shouted in shock.

"My thoughts exactly. I know French breads are tough but bloody hell I didn't think it would go through the back of his head!" Nick replied.

"What the fuck were you thinking? I was dealing with it; you didn't have to do that!" Tony shouted angrily.

"Maybe, but he was a dead man walking and we haven't got time to sit around waiting for him to conk it just so we can kill him. It's better this way for all of us and you didn't have to get your hands dirty so technically I did you a favour. Come on Tone, let's get the baby supplies and bugger off. When we leave, keep your eyes out for that van he described. What was it he said? A blue 55 plate Citroen Relay wasn't it? If we get the opportunity we should take it. I know I said we don't need the van but all that booze and fags does not belong with the bastards that left this poor sod here to die. They deserve to be drank and smoked by better folk than that. Folk like me! Oh and you of course. Come on, let's get cracking!" Nick said, moving to retrieve a nearby shopping trolley.

Tony looked upon the fallen Andy and the bloodied stale French bread protruding from his mouth. Although he could understand why Nick did what he did, he did not believe it to be right and felt that the choice of how he was to die belonged to Andy. Nick's actions re-assured him that his decision to leave was the right one and as soon as the opportunity presented itself, he would be gone and without Nick's knowledge if possible. But for now, he needed his new volatile companion and the shelter he promised. He was tired, cold and hungry with the prospect of resting at the forefront of his mind. So he helped his unstable acquaintance to fill a shopping trolley with as much baby formula, nappies, sterilising tablets, wipes and medicine as it could hold, then they left the supermarket travelling back towards Churchill Mansions, Nick singing Terrorvision songs and Tony quietly following behind, mindful of how vulnerable and exposed they were.

"Here we are Tone, home sweet home," Nick said with a pride filled smile, arms wide, looking up to Churchill Mansions and the splattered zombies that surrounded it.

The entrance to the high rise apartment building was surrounded by large iron fencing. Nick removed a chain from around his neck. Attached to it was a set of keys which he used to unlock a padlock that secured the gates. He pushed the shopping trolley through. Tony following cautiously, watching Nick's every move.

"You see not only have I surrounded the building with the dead but it's protected by this iron fencing too. For zombies it's mission impossible. The dead will hide our smell and, should that fail, this strong fencing will keep them out. Yep, we will be alright here for a long time I reckon. There's no reason why we can't see this thing out in relative comfort. Me you and the girls, our own little post-apocalyptic family. Hey it'll be like The Walton's only with more booze and swearing. Not in front of the girls though eh Tone?" he continued, replacing the padlock and the key chain around his neck.

Tony looked at the fencing. Could it be climbed? Possibly but not unaided. When he was to leave he would need the key to unlock the gate. Maybe Nick would soon pass out from his heavy drinking and he could remove it without him noticing. The next chance he had, that key chain was his.

They entered the entrance hall of the building. It was dark with furniture from the ground floor apartments stacked up against windows.

"Going up," Nick said, depressing the button for the building's elevator which arrived promptly.

He pushed the trolley inside and pressed the button for the top floor then turned to Tony, whose concern at the prospect of using the elevator was evident.

"Don't worry we're taking the stairs. We'll meet the lift at the top. If it does conk out at least all we've lost is the supplies. It's a death trap that thing, always breaking down and I tell you what, I wouldn't want to be stuck inside when the power goes out. Trapped in a small dark room with no way out slowly starving to death? Hey if that was ever to happen and I died first you have my permission to eat me. Anything for you Tone. I'll write it down on a bit of paper when we get upstairs so it's all official like, OK? Come on then..." Nick said, taking the first steps of the long climb.

Tony's legs tired quickly and he sat for a moment. He had only walked a few flights and could feel his calves constrict as if someone was reaching through his skin and gripping the muscle tight. He could hear Nick, several flights ahead of him, happily chattering away, planning out how their living arrangements would work.

"So this is what we'll do. Me and the kids will have the top floor and you can have the one below us. We can share the supplies out between us. The thing about this building, Tone, is all the residents were knocking on a bit and you know what old people are like for hoarding food don't you? There's enough grub in this place to last 3 zombie apocalypses. Apocalypses, apocali, apocalees... what's the plural for more than one end of the world? Oh I don't fucking care! It's the baby that's the problem really. Our bounty from the Co-Op should keep us going for a while. No doubt we'll have to go out again, further afield next time I reckon. But there's plenty of cars around and I've seen Gone in 60 Seconds like 50 times so hot wiring one should be a piece of piss. Oh it's gonna be great. There's a Karaoke machine in one of the apartments and I've got a load of CD's in my Nan's. I'm sure there's some

Terrorvision in there. Once you've had a rest maybe you can belt out a few numbers? The kids would love that..."

"What the hell have I gotten myself into?" Tony said to himself, rubbing warmth into his calves before continuing the climb.

When he finally reached the top floor he found Nick stood quiet at an open apartment doorway looking in. He joined him to see what had caught his attention. The doorway led to a living room and on the couch slept a young girl of no more than 8 years of age. In her arms she cradled a baby.

"Meet Sophie and baby Gaby. I'll put the shopping away and sort some milk out for the little one. You make yourself at home. It's good to have you with us Tone. Together I think we can really give these girls a chance," Nick said sincerely before leaving to take the trolley to the apartment's kitchen.

Tony walked to the girls and knelt down in front of them. They looked so peaceful and innocent unlike the world he had awoken to that morning. Gaby began to stir, her sister's long brown hair tickling her face. He reached to remove it but on touching the hair, Sophie opened her eyes.

"You're going to die tomorrow!" she said quickly before closing her eyes and falling back to sleep.

Tony went cold on hearing her words and fell backwards in shock. What made her say it he did not know and he did not want to be around should she wake and say it again.

He walked to the kitchen area where Nick was sterilising baby bottles.

"Hey up Tone, fancy a brew? Kettle's over there or if you want something harder there's lager in the fridge and plenty more Jack Daniels in the cupboard, just make yourself at home. This is your place now too. Hey later on maybe you could give us all a sing song, the little ones will love that. There are a couple of guitars in one of the apartments so we could have a jam too! I mean I'm not as good as you but I can hold my own," Nick said excitedly.

"The girl, Sophie? She err, she just spoke," Tony said, visibly shaken.

"She said you were going to die didn't she? She said the same to me too. I wouldn't worry so much. Poor kid has been through a lot in a short space of time. Grief affects us all in different ways. Look at me, I killed my Nan and I haven't been sober since!" Nick said with a drunken grin.

Tony didn't reply, instead he left Nick preparing the baby milk and went in search of somewhere to rest his head, being careful not to wake Sophie and Gaby as he left the apartment.

Remembering what his intoxicated host had said, he walked down the stairway to the apartment below. Its layout was identical to Nick's – a large living area with separate kitchen and a doorway leading to a bedroom. He surmised that a man lived here, and a lonely one too. He could see that from the tired furniture which consisted of two deck chairs and a foot rest pointing at an old black and white television set. Old military pictures, empty bottles of real ale and heavy dust completed the scene. He entered the kitchen and inspected the cupboards. They were stocked fully with long life tinned foods such as corned beef, beans, processed fruit and stewed steak. The fridge was void of anything edible and was instead filled with bottled water. Whoever lived here had been preparing to see this thing out.

He opened the door to the bedroom. Inside, a single mattress lay on the floor, thick with dirt and yellow and brown stains. Also in the room was a telescope positioned to look through the bedroom window and next to it a desk with an open journal, a laptop and C.B. equipment on top. He took the journal and exited the room, shutting the door behind him.

It was a beautiful journal, bound in a deep blue leather with imprints of stars and planets. On the reverse of the cover, written in ink it said

"Property of Trust No One: Aliens of Runcorn Spotters Elite"

He started to read. It was an account of Trust No One's nightly star watchings and reports of strange objects in the sky over the town. There was even newspaper cuttings detailing eye witness accounts of cylinder shaped objects hovering over the River Mersey, sucking up the water. There were transcripts of conversations with other members of Aliens of Runcorn Spotters Elite. Members such as Sky Watcher and Lone Wolf. It was whilst reading through a transcript he realised what the acronym for this group was. A.R.S.E. They were all members of a secret group of alien enthusiasts called A.R.S.E! Tony couldn't contain himself and fell to the floor in a fit of laughter. He giggled so hard he could barely breathe. In an attempt to regain control he thought about all the horrible things he had seen that day from waking inside a plane wreck, the rabid geese, watching Mike transform into the Undead, Andy with a French loaf sticking out of his mouth and the chilling prediction of death from Sophie, but nothing could calm his laughter. He knew it wasn't even that funny but the thought of people calling themselves A.R.S.E was too much and there was no coming back. He would have to see it through.

After what felt like hours, his laughing fit subsided and he lay on the floor exhausted. With heavy eyes he drifted into a sleep with the journal in his hand and began dreaming of home. His dreams took him back to being a child at Christmas with family all around, sleeping with bellies full from his mother's festive feast. His granddad, mother, father and sister all lay slouched wearing paper party hats, snoring as Queen Elizabeth II delivered her Christmas Speech on the television.

Tony sat on the floor playing with his toys. He looked to his snoozing family and felt blessed and full of love. Then he noticed something, a small rip in the flesh under his mother's eye. He watched as it split and opened wider. Then another tear appeared on her cheek, then her neck and on her forehead. He looked to his other family and the same was happening to them and lesions broke out across their bodies splitting their skin.

His nightmare continued as out of the wounds slithered thick black worms. Young Tony was frightened and quickly scurried backwards, bumping up against his television set where Queen Elizabeth II was still addressing her public. If he'd looked around he would have noticed that she had transformed into the undead and now wore a crown fashioned from human hands and a gown made from the skinned faces of Mike Green, Gary Littlemore, Andy Deen, Nick Fieldsend and the girls Sophie and Gaby.

"Nobody can save you now," she screeched.

Her arms reached through the television set and wrapped around him, dragging him screaming through the TV screen.

He woke from his nightmare eyes wide and unable to breath due to the large hand that choked his throat. A heavy set man lent over him, positioning his large round face close to his, exposing his crooked and yellow plaque stained teeth. The man breathed heavily, the smell of stale cigarettes and coffee filled Tony's crinkled nose. Behind the man, he could see an elderly, thin woman with short grey hair and skin similar to cracked leather.

"You should have stayed upstairs!" the woman said.

The woman reached down to Tony's face and with a mutilated zombie hand, scratched a bloodied fingernail across his face, tearing the flesh.

With his free hand the heavy set man slipped a knife deep into Tony's stomach and began tearing through his skin, ripping his abdomen wide open. The elderly, thin woman watched on, an evil grin creasing her gaunt face.

Tony felt nothing, only warmth as he slipped from life. His final thoughts lay with Sophie and her prediction of his death. The man moved away from Tony's lifeless body and stood next to the woman. Together they started to count.

"1, 2, 3, 4, 5, 6, 7…"

They had barely counted for two minutes before Tony's body started to twitch.

"Interesting," the woman said, "very interesting. Almost half the time it took for the last one to turn. Now what did we do differently? They're a similar build and height. I broke their skin with your daddy's hand and you stabbed them both in the same place. Age! Age is the difference. This one is younger than the last that has to be it. Finish him son, he's served his purpose."

The man walked over to Tony and looking into his white glazed eyes he stabbed the knife hard through his forehead, killing him for a second time. He looked up to the ceiling as the muffled sounds of a Karaoke machine could be heard. The song was Oblivion by Terrovision and the man singing was murdering it.

He retracted the knife from Tony's forehead and smiled.

"Momma?" he said to the elderly, thin woman in a drawn out deep dull voice.

"Not just yet son. We'll let the idiot think he's alone for now. He'll come looking for his friend soon enough. We must be patient and take our chance when presented. What have I always told you?" she asked.

"Good things come to those who wait?" he replied, his deep rumbling tone suited his large frame perfectly.

"That's right. Dispose of the body, he's already stinking up the place. Then we'll get some rest," she said.

The man lifted Tony's body with little effort, opened the apartment window and pushed him through, sending him falling to the hard concrete outside. The elderly woman placed her arm around her son and walked him to the bedroom, playing with his hair and humming the lullaby Rockabye Baby.

Journal Entry 11

With Emily and Jonathon in charge of finishing off fortifying Diant basecamp, I took the opportunity to take a shower. Man it felt good to have the hot water rush over my body. Maybe it was being outside in the cold all morning, maybe it was the thought of washing away the memories of all the horrible things I had seen, done, touched and stepped in since the zombies came, or maybe it was knowing that this near scalding hot shower could very well be the last one I took. Who knows how long the power is going to last? Shit it could have cut out there and then and I would have been left stark naked freezing my bollocks off whilst stumbling around trying to find a towel with my eyes full of soap. Thankfully that didn't happen and I was enjoying one of the greatest showers of my life.

There's something about the sudden change in temperature from shivering cold to boiling hot that causes my body to slip into complete relaxation. The only thing that would have made it perfect was if I was having a bath instead. But there was not a chance in hell that I was going to lie down in my brother's tub. It had more limescale and dirt than Bigfoot's shitter. It was difficult enough to stand in it never mind take a soak and so you can put my decision into perspective just remember, I've had my feet inside of a zombie's head.

As the bathroom filled with steam, visibility became restricted to the point that I could no longer see my hand in front of my face. With piping hot water hitting my skin, the sensation was truly blissful. Muscle by muscle I felt the tension ease from my body and I allowed myself to drift, to take myself away from the hell that was now my life. No zombies and no death, just complete relaxation. I took myself back to when Emily was born, to what it felt like witnessing my daughter arrive into this world. To hold her close. To watch as her tiny hand wrapped around my finger, gripping it tightly. To look upon my partner Sarah, her face beaming with pride. Even after a long and exhausting labour she had never looked so beautiful. Then I recalled the moment she looked back at me, smiled her perfect smile and said "We did it" before closing her eyes and falling into a sleep she would never wake from.

You know, I think that is the first time I have ever told anyone other than my brother and daughter what happened that day. How Sarah, my long term girlfriend and mother to my daughter, was taken from us. I'm not sure why I never told anyone. I suppose I thought it was nobody's business. Things seem kinda different now and if, as Butty thinks, people will read this journal when hell is over, I feel I should be as truthful as possible. Doctors said she contracted an infection during pregnancy that went undetected and that it was extremely rare for such a thing to happen. Their explanation was as good as a shrug of the shoulders as far as I was concerned. Nothing about what happened to Sarah made sense or could be explained. Not to me anyway. I just wasn't prepared to listen and I wasn't for a long time.

For many years, that image of Sarah smiling at me and saying "We did it" haunted me. Whenever I closed my eyes I saw her face. As soon as I woke, went to work, played with Emily... no matter what it was I was doing, her face was always there and it was agony. Everything I did reminded me of her and at times I even found myself begging to God for the memory of Sarah to disappear, to be erased from my life forever. People say that time is a great healer and they are right, it is. But do you know what else is a great healer? Being a father. As Emily grew I recognised more and more of her mother in her, in her mannerisms, her fussiness over food and in her smile. That smile was the turning point for me. How could I look upon my daughter smiling her mother's perfect smile and feel pain and hatred? I now understood that what happened to Sarah could not be undone and, more importantly, that nobody was to blame. Sarah may be gone but she is still very much alive within Emily. Once I had realised that, the memory of Emily's birth and Sarah looking at me smiling for the last time was no longer something that haunted me. I began to cherish that memory and I have visited it often over the years. Whenever I feel alone and whenever I need comfort, all I have to do is close my eyes and my world is again whole. With everything that had happened since yesterday I was glad to have that memory to call upon.

I was lost within my happy place, enjoying again being with my daughter and the love of my life, when a deathly smell dragged me back to reality. Through the thick steam that engulfed my brother's bathroom an evil scent filled my nostrils. I feared the worst, believing the undead had somehow managed to breech DIANT Basecamp. I turned off the shower taps and gingerly stepped out of the grotty bath tub, reaching around in the hope of finding something I could use to protect myself. There was nothing but I did find the door handle and quickly opened it with a view to making my escape. On pulling the door open, the bathroom steam escaped through it so fast I felt a breeze brush against the back of my cooling wet legs. I swear it was as if it wanted out of that bathroom more than I did. Out on the hallway I spied my daughter's hockey stick which I quickly grabbed then tentatively moved back towards the bathroom, placing my back against the wall next to its open doorway. Two thoughts ran through my mind. First and foremost I was thinking of the potential threat and if there indeed was a zombie in the bathroom, how I was going to take care of it. My other thought was of Emily and Jonathon. Were they OK? If they were then I hoped to God neither of them walked out onto the hallway now, especially Emily. The last thing any daughter needs to see is her father naked.

It had to be a zombie. The smell coming through the open doorway was so bad only the undead could be responsible. With the steam sufficiently dispersed now was as good a time as any to make a move. I took a deep breath and let out what I hoped would be a menacing war cry but in reality sounded more like Robin Gibb warbling out a Bee Gees number. I ran into the bathroom like a screaming banshee, swinging Emily's hockey stick like a maniac but to my surprise I hit nothing. I opened my eyes (I know I know, it's a miracle I've stayed alive this long) to see the bathroom was empty. But the smell, fuck me it was stronger than ever. Where the hell was it coming from? I scanned the room. Apart from the grime and dirt that already coated the walls, ceiling, floor, sink and tub there was nothing I could see to lay blame to the hideous stink. Then my gaze fixed on the toilet and the old wooden lid that was hiding any content. I realised something was in there because steam was escaping from the small gap between the porcelain toilet rim and the wooden seat. I lifted the lid and it was like opening Pandora's Box. Unlike Pandora's Box which contained hate, envy and every illness, disease and bad thing known to man, my brother's toilet housed the biggest turd I have ever seen. I mean it was bigger than a house brick. King Kong would have shed a tear squeezing this one out. When I first entered the bathroom, before taking a shower, the room had felt arctic. The cold air must have frozen the mammoth shit timber but then having the shower run so hot had thawed it out, unleashing its whiff. Only one man could have been responsible for this and I think we both know who that is. 80s Dave aka Dump Truck, the filthy bastard. He could have bloody flushed the thing! Although, looking at the size of his deposit I'm not surprised he didn't. It really would have tested the plumbing. I had to grab a coat hanger from my brother's bedroom and prod at the humongous turd till it was broken up enough to flush. By the time I was done I felt like I needed another shower!

Dried and dressed but with the whiff of the bathroom still tickling my nose hairs, I walked out onto the hallway. My intention was to check on Emily and Jonathon and how they were progressing with securing the house when I noticed the door leading down to the cellar was open. This struck me as strange as since we arrived here yesterday, none of us had ventured to the ground floor of the house and I was sure I had noticed it was closed before I took my shower. I can even remember Butty telling me he had secured the cellar. My brother had removed the staircase leading to the ground floor as an added security measure. He had also moved all essentials to the first floor so there was no need for any of us to go down there. So why was the door open? I had to investigate and again I took my daughter's hockey stick for protection before carefully climbing down to the ground floor.

I cautiously walked towards the open doorway. With both hands wrapped tightly around the hockey stick, I was as prepared as I could be should I find myself confronted with intruders. The chance of there being zombies in the cellar was slim at best. The door to the house remained both closed and secured as did all of the windows. If the undead had attacked then I would expect to see evidence of a forced entry, shredded skin and blood. That's the thing about zombies, they're not very good at covering up their tracks. People on the other hand, well people are sneaky bastards and if anyone knew that Butty had two generators plus a lifetimes supply of tinned spam in the cellar, then I wouldn't put it past them taking a chance on a shifty steal.

I stood at the top of the stairs looking down at the steep concrete steps. The cellar was brightly lit which left me convinced that there was definitely someone down there. There is no way Butty would leave a light on in a room that was not being used. It was one of his pet hates and, as children, running into rooms and turning lights on was the source of much amusement for me and much annoyance and frustration for Butty. I recall this one time when he was looking after me whilst Nan and Granddad had gone out for a dance and a game of bingo at the Runcorn War Memorial Social Club. I spent the best part of the evening running around the house flicking light switch after light swift. On, off, on, off the lights flickered. Like a budget rave without any music. Our grandparents came home to find my brother had twisted my arms behind my back and super glued my hands together. Granddad had to soak my hands in my Nan's nail polish remover to free them up. To this day I don't have any finger prints on both hands because of this. Maybe I should have pursued a life of crime instead of eating disgusting mayonnaise for a living eh? I'll tell you one thing, I've never left a light on in an empty room since!

I gently placed my right foot on the top step then slowly began my descent. Thoughts of disturbing a gang of thieving survivors looting my brother's stash of apocalypse necessities rattled through my tired mind. Christ, all I had to defend myself was Emily's hockey stick. No doubt the intruders would be violent. If they had the balls to loot an occupied house then surely they wouldn't think twice about attacking someone, especially a trembling wreck of a man wielding a teenage girl's hockey stick.

Every carefully placed step brought more and more of the cellar into my line of sight. The bright light cast a long dark shadow across the floor. It was of a man and a huge one at that if his shadow was anything to go by. I gulped hard. The hockey stick began to slip from my grip due to the nervous sweat that seemed to be running from every pore in my body. I'd need another shower at this rate! I started to question what the hell it was I thought I was doing. I'm not my brother and I'm not 80s Dave. I'm not even Emily! I'm just a man with an irrational hatred of mayonnaise and the gag reflex of Linda Blair in The Exorcist. This wasn't the kind of thing I did and as I continued to try and talk myself out of entering the basement, my legs did not appear to be listening to my protests and before I knew it I was stood in the cellar, looking upon the back of a young man, knelt down, quietly sobbing into his hands. It was Jonathon.

I let out an involuntary sigh of relief which alerted Jonathon to my presence. He quickly dried his eyes and rose to his feet, obviously startled by my presence. I too was surprised to see him down here, albeit pleasantly. Thank the heavens his looming shadow was a red herring.

"Mr Diant you, you startled me. What are you doing down here?" An agitated Jonathon jittered.

"I saw the door open and thought we had intruders. You're lucky I noticed it was you or you could have had this hockey stick wrapped around your head," I replied, acting the tough guy. "Why are you down here anyway? There's nothing here but tins of spam and these old generators,"

It was clear he was upset and had been crying for some time. His tears had cleaned away the dirt from his cheeks; the rest of his face was still marked with soil and grime from hammering stakes into the ground outside the house. I was reluctant to comment on his upset in case he did not want to share what plagued him.

"I wanted to go somewhere quiet away from everyone. Somewhere I could be on my own for a little while. I had thought to lock myself away in the bathroom but someone had left a shit the size of the Titanic in the toilet so I couldn't stay in there. Did you see me crying? You did didn't you? Please don't tell Emily Mr Diant. I don't want her to know I've been crying. She's so strong and in control. I've tried to be like her but it's difficult you know? I haven't seen my parents for over a day now and no matter how hard I try to put it to the back of my mind and carry on as normal I can't, I just can't. I'm not an idiot. I know they are probably dead. Do you know how difficult that is? To know I'll never see them again? It's all I can think about. You know the last thing I did was complain to my mum because she hadn't ironed my favourite shirt and I wanted to look nice for Emily. I walked out on her angry over a stupid shirt. I keep playing it over and over in my mind. I would do anything to change what happened, anything to take away how horrible I was to her and instead give her hug and tell her how much I love her. Then there's my Dad. I had been a real shit to him for weeks. He would always nag and get on to me about school and making plans for when I left. I'm a teenager! I don't want to think about that stuff, I just want to live in the now and spend time with Emily. When I think about how I dismissed everything he said I feel sick. He only wanted what's best and I was too selfish to see that," Jonathon cried.

I felt really bad for the kid. He was falling apart in front of me and all I wanted to do was tell him everything would be ok but how could I? The world we had known was gone. Death, chaos, pain and fear had taken the places of comfort, security, protection and happiness. His family was gone and he never had a chance to say goodbye. That was something I could relate to as I had felt the same when Sarah was taken from me. The best I could do was to let Jonathon know that he was wanted and how much he means to our little group.

"I know what it's like to lose someone suddenly without having a chance to say goodbye. Without having the chance to tell them one last time how much you love them and how much they mean to you. Believe me when I say I understand what you are going through. When it comes to people we love it's easy to think we have all the time in the world to say those things. You think they'll be around forever. Life is precious, especially now, and you have to concentrate on what you have. What you have is Emily and the rest of us lunatics. We might not be your family but I can tell you this - we're the next best thing. Emily loves you, I can see that clearly and if it wasn't for you, she might not be alive. Shit, I might not be alive. I have you to thank for that. You are an integral part of our little team and if we're going to keep kicking this apocalypse in its bum hole then we need you to be strong. Emily needs you to be strong. You're wrong with what you said before. You're every bit as tough as my daughter. She's like she is because she's got you. Yeah ok, her Uncle Butty brainwashing her these past few years has probably got something to do with it too but you're good for her. You're good for each other and I for one am glad she met you. Even if you do need a haircut and have suspect taste in jeans," I said, placing my arm around his shoulder, giving him a good old man hug.

Whilst my words couldn't erase Jonathon's loss it did cheer him up momentarily. He even managed a smile at my quip about his hair and jeans.

"Thanks Mr. Diant, that means a lot," Jonathon replied. "You know, there's more than just these generators down here."

Jonathon nodded towards a large plastic beer keg up against the far wall. Written across the keg in a childish scribble in black biro were the words "Butty's Brew". Now normally I would never condone underage drinking. But with everything he had been through, if anyone deserved a drink it was Jonathon.

"Fill your boots," I said, motioning for him to approach the keg and take a drink. "Just don't tell Butty I said you could drink his home brew. He's very precious about that stuff."

He placed his head under the keg tap and opened the valve. A dark brown ale gushed out, overwhelming the poor lad's throat.

"Christ it tastes like feet!" Jonathon coughed and spluttered.

"That will be the cheese. He's been obsessed with making the perfect cheese flavoured beer for years. Brie Bitter, Mascarpone Mild, Cheddar Artois... he's tried them all but could never get the flavour right. He said he was saving this batch for a special occasion so maybe he's cracked it this time," I said.

"Well if the flavour he was looking for was athletes foot then he got it spot on. Whoa it's strong though. It's got a definite kick to it. I can feel the heat burning through my chest," replied Jonathon before positioning his mouth under the tap and chugging down more of the cheesy brew.

"Hey go easy on that stuff. We don't want Butty to notice that someone has been at his home brew. He'll probably subject us all to an evening of interrogations and torture methods till the culprit, i.e. you, confessed. I for one don't fancy spending my night being subjected to Chinese burn after Chinese burn whilst my nutty brother sings the theme tune to the Golden Girls," I said.

The threat of Butty's torture method put an end to Jonathon's beer guzzling and we made our way out of the cellar and back upstairs. My words had helped, if not only for a short while, to lift Jonathon out of his slump and when he saw Emily cooking up a spam dinner in Butty's bedroom/kitchen, he brightened up and a smile spread across his face big enough to warm the coldest of hearts.

Scabby Heads & 80s Threads

"We shouldn't have left him," Joni jittered, fidgeting nervously whilst scratching the dry raw scalp of his bald head. "He's our colleague, ONE OF US! We're supposed to look out for each other, especially now. Thanks to you guys we left him to die. TO DIE! Christ he saved my life yesterday. I was done for, finished and he was there when I needed him and when he needed me what did I do? Nothing. I did fucking nothing because you two dragged me out of there! You know what? I'd take Andy over either of you fucking losers. Ged won't be happy when he finds out what went down. He won't be happy at all and when he wants to know what happened to Andy I'm telling him the truth. That you guys made the decision to leave him behind and I had nothing to do with it. This is all on you! Even if, even if I was involved, Ged's my family, he's my cousin. He'd go easy on me anyway but not you guys. You guys are for it when we get back. Remember what he did to that old lady? Well that's nothing in comparison to what he will do to you, you pair of shits. For fuck's sake my arse hurts!" he complained, the neck of a vodka bottle pushing into his tailbone. "Drive carefully over speed bumps will you? It's not exactly comfortable sitting back here. Why the hell do I have to sit in the back anyway? I never get to sit up front."

"We, we don't want you sitting up front Joni because you, you never stop bitching and you are always itching that manky head of yours huhuhuh. You're like a human snow globe huhuhuh," Tom giggled his response from the passenger seat of the van.

Tom Morrell pushed his chubby dirty fingers into an open tin of corned beef then shovelled the content into his mouth, eating greedily before licking every last piece from his grotty fat digits. It was the third tin he had devoured since hastily leaving the Co-operative supermarket on Granville Street. He was a big man with a big appetite and corned beef was his favourite. Tom was ecstatic when Ged told them they would be going out to find supplies. He knew he would be able to help himself to as much food as he liked. He was a basic man, tall with a large frame, strong and responded well to instruction. As long as there was food to eat he could be controlled and Ged knew how to exploit the big guy's weakness for his own gains.

Ed Crothers placed his left hand on the gear stick and awkwardly shifted into 5th. He had never driven Andy's van before and it had long been an annoyance of his that his now deceased work mate refused to let anyone behind the wheel. With Andy gone, there was nothing to stop him and he was enjoying the drive, relishing in the fact that his colleague would be going berserk if he was still alive.

He lifted his eyes from the road, looking into the rear view mirror of the Blue 55 plate Citroen Relay, frowning at the sight of Joni continuing to complain and scratch at his repulsive head in the back of the van. His protesting had been continuous since they had all witnessed Andy Deen get attacked by zombies at the Co-operative Supermarket and had left him for dead.

It was Ed's decision to leave Andy behind and he knew it to be the right one. Having already been bitten, his colleague was a dead man walking and Joni's threat of blabbing to the boss was not a concern. Ed had worked for Ged long enough to know that he would have acted exactly the same if he had been in his position. Plus, it was only yesterday that Ged was considering 'ending' Andy himself. He had nothing to fear from his boss, of that he was sure. If it had been Joni they left behind then it would have been a very different story.

"Why couldn't it have been Joni we had to leave behind hey Ed huh?" Tom asked, spitting pieces of corned beef across the dashboard.

"No such luck Tom. Anyway he's Ged's cousin, our lives wouldn't be worth living if we let anything happen to him. Even if he is the world's biggest pain in the arse. The fidgeting, whingeing little shit is our responsibility. If he dies, we die," Ed replied, grabbing an old rag and wiping the chewed corned beef from the dashboard. "Come on now Tom have some respect, this is Andy's van you're spitting your corned beef all over. Now how would he feel if he knew you were making a mess like this?"

"But Andy is dead now Ed. He doesn't feel anything anymore?" Came Tom's confused reply.

Ed could not help but laugh at the response and Tom, still confused at Ed's question, started to laugh also. He wasn't so sure why he was laughing but if Ed found something funny then so did he. This incensed Joni and from his position in the rear of the van, he yelled and protested at the chortling coming from up front. Ed and Tom curbed their laughter. If only to shut him up.

"Will Ged be mad at us Ed, for what we did? We had no choice right, you said it, we had no choice. The bad people got to him and we had to leave him. Once the bad people get you, you go to Heaven where Mum and Uncle Lenny went and you leave your body behind and it becomes one of the bad people. You taught me that Ed," Tom said.

"That's right Tom. These bad people that you see, they are not like you and I. They used to be but they died and all the things that made them human… compassion, empathy, courage, fear… they all went to heaven. Only their bodies remained and they got taken over by the bad people and all they want to do is hurt you. What do you do if you see the bad people Tom?" Ed asked.

"I don't do nothing unless they get close then I smash their heads until they break," Tom replied.

"That's right and don't you worry about Ged. I'll explain what happened and if he is mad then it won't be with you. You got nothing to worry about, trust me," Ed explained, attempting to ease the big guy's concerns.

"You've got everything to worry about you big dumb idiot!" Joni shouted from the back of the van.

Tom lowered his head and sulked into his chest, scooping the final chunks of corned beef into his mouth. No sooner had Ed picked Tom up, Joni had knocked him back down again. Ed was furious but held himself in a silent rage knowing that one day, Joni was going to pay for his behaviour and Ed said a little prayer for it to be sooner rather than later.

"This is the last stop of the day. Let's take what we can quickly so we can get back to Ged. He'll be wondering where the hell we are," Ed said, bringing the van to a stop outside a small row of shops on Russell Road in the Weston Point area of Runcorn.

"Don't bark orders at me, Crothers, who the fuck do you think you're talking to? I'm in charge here not you and I get to say if this is the last stop!" Joni yelled.

Joni's forehead tightened from frowning, such was his anger, and puss wheezed from an open sore, dripping down into his left eye.

"Eeeeeeee....!" Tom repulsed, pointing his chubby index finger at the pink ooze sliding into Joni's eye.

"You know what? FUCK THE BOTH OF YOU! Do what you want, I'm staying here in the van. I hope you both get yourselves fucking killed you pair of cunts!" Joni screamed.

The insults continued as Joni flew into a rage, punching and kicking the insides of the van. Ed and Tom left him to it, grabbing baseball bats for weapons and leaving the vehicle which shook back and forth with the muffled sounds of Joni's tantrum audible from outside. There were zombies everywhere but non showed interest in them, instead they shuffled towards Sandy Lane, in the direction of the Pavilions.

"Remember what I said now; ignore the bad people, only attack if you need to defend yourself, you got that?" Ed asked his friend.

"Uh-huh," came Tom's nervous reply.

"The two that run this newsagent are good people; I have been coming here for years. James Haste served me my first bottle of cider when I was just eighteen and Kerrie Ross has worked there for as long as I can remember. If they are still alive then maybe we can work something out and they will let us take some supplies. If they're dead then, well, we take everything," Ed said.

They quickly made their way to the newsagents. Ed pulled open the shop door and they cautiously walked inside. The first thing that hit him was the smell. It was a mixture of sickly sweet and decaying meat. Like rotting skin sprayed with cheap perfume. The smell of the dead. Ed knew what it meant. It meant James and Kerrie had not survived, but had they remained dead or had they come back? He turned to check on Tom who was filling his pockets with confectionery, completely oblivious to the smell and Ed's concern.

Ed slowly and with caution moved forward until he reached the back of the shop. That's where he found what was responsible for the smell. Slumped against the store room door was Kerrie. She was dead and by her own hands. Around her neck was a noose made from a washing line. The other end was tied to a broken light fitting. She had hung herself, the light fitting eventually giving way. Written on the store room door it said...

Do not open!

Zombie inside.

Forgive me James.

Ed nervously placed his ear against the door expecting to hear the heavy groaning of a zombie inside. He wasn't disappointed and no sooner had his ear touched the cold wooden door, the undead James Haste attacked, slamming hard against the door over and over. Ed backed away, returning to Tom at the front of the shop. He had no intention of telling his friend what he had found. Tom was content in his happy place, eating and stuffing his pockets with as much chocolate as he could. There was no reason to spook him.

Grabbing several carrier bags from behind the counter, Ed filled them with anything he thought would be useful. Flu medicines, headache pills, bottled water, toilet roll, bin bags, matches and lighters all found their way into the bags. He only paused his looting when he caught Tom removing his recently acquired sweets from his pockets and shoving them into his mouth.

"What are you doing Tom?" Ed asked.

"There's no room left in my pockets for anymore snacks so I have to eat what's in there to make space for more. It's a vicious circle!" Tom mumbled, jelly sweets and chocolate spluttering from his mouth.

Ed smiled at his friend's reasoning then offered him several empty carrier bags.

"Here you big goof ball. Fill these with as much as you can. I think when we get back I'll keep hold of this stuff for you. You'll soon be the size of a tank if I don't," Ed said.

"That's a good thing Ed. Bad people can't hurt a tank and I can just drive right over them!" Tom said, getting down on all fours and pointing his right arm out straight, roaming around the shop doing his best tank impression.

They both fell about laughing. Tom's innocence was a blessing for Ed and he always managed to put a smile on his face no matter how bad things were. Their laughter was short lived though as the sound of someone shouting outside could be heard.

"Fuck me Ace, did you hear his head crack against the floor? If he's not dead then Gary Numan isn't the greatest musician of all time!"

"He's not dead."

"Isn't he? Well then forget everything I just said."

Ed and Tom looked through the shop window to see the rear doors of the van open and Joni lying face down in the road, blood tricking from his bald scabby head. Standing over him were two men. One was carrying a large plastic spoon and wearing headphones with sunglasses covering his eyes. The other was holding a crowbar and had a lampshade around his neck. Behind them, further along the road was a 1980s Ford Thunderbird.

"It's his own fault. What was the crazy bastard thinking? Leaping out at us like that."

"He must have got his foot caught when he jumped."

They watched as the men discussed what had happened to Joni then proceeded to transfer the loot from the van to the Ford Thunderbird.

A plan started to formulate in Ed's mind. A way for them to be rid of Joni for good and return to Ged without him holding them responsible for his cousin's demise. He just needed to wait for the men to leave so he and Tom could make their move and convince a couple of zombies to feed on Joni's scab covered body.

_____

Dave slouched against the bonnet of the Ford Thunderbird. Taking in a long pull of his cigarette, he gazed along the icy road, bright sunlight reflected off the glistening frost covered tarmac. It was eerie quiet with nothing to see except the dead starlings and pigeons that lay frozen. He shifted his eyes to the right, looking out across Runcorn, towards the River Mersey, Widnes and further afield to Merseyside and the city of Liverpool. He could see for miles from his position. The many fires that had illuminated the sky the previous night still burnt strong, filling the skyline with thick black smoke. Beyond the smoke he could make out the distant shape of Liverpool Cathedral. The fifth largest Cathedral in the world, it has a height of 331 feet and its tower can be seen for miles around. He closed his eyes and let his mind carry him there and observe what he imagined was happening.

Hordes of zombies surrounded the cathedral, their hands reaching skyward to the many survivors that had secured themselves on the roof of the building. The dead kept coming, moaning and groaning as they trampled over each other, desperate to reach the people up high. Their persistent pursuit of the survivors was building a growing wall and slowly but surely the bricks of the cathedral became obscured by rotting flesh. The survivors on top were doomed and, taking suicide over being eaten alive, one by one they jumped to their deaths.

"Poor fuckers!" Dave said, shaking himself free from his hellish daydream.

Finishing his smoke he looked inside his cigarette packet for another. All he found was a few lonely cigarettes. Being low on tabs always made him feel anxious.

"Come on Butty lad!" he moaned.

"Almost there," came the laboured response.

Dave looked to the stone steps leading down to Butty's house. First, his head was visible, then his face, then the lampshade covering his neck and then finally the rest of Butty in his homemade Zombie armour. He struggled to the top of the steps, carrying two large duffle bags, both bulging at the seams. It was a long and ridiculous reveal and Dave could not contain the belly laugh that followed.

"Laugh it up Dave, but if we come under attack from zombies it will be me who's laughing big man," Butty said.

"I doubt it lar, I've seen tortoises move faster than you. You couldn't outrun a slug never mind a zombie. What's in the bags Power Stranger?" Dave replied with a smile.

"Funny, are you like this with everyone?" Butty asked.

"Not everyone. Usually it takes me months of sussing someone out to see if they are worthy of my insults. Just ask your John. It took me the best part of six months for me to decide he was good enough. Don't get me wrong, I always knew he was a top lad but it wasn't till one day in work when I caught him humming the theme tune to The Greatest American Hero that I decided we were going to be buddies. I've been insulting him ever since! These days though, current circumstances do not allow me six months to weigh someone up so I've had to adapt. You should be honoured really because even though you are nuttier than a Walnut Whip, I've decided I like you anyway. So come on then Butty lad, let's have it, what's in the bags?" Dave asked.

"Protection, let's just leave it at that," Butty replied.

Dave thought it best not to press him for an answer. If Butty didn't want to discuss what was in the duffle bags then he reasoned it must be pretty bad. Instead, he helped him place the bags in the boot of the car before they entered the vehicle.

"Smoke before we leave, Ace?" Dave offered, handing Butty one of his remaining cigarettes.

"No thanks, not with this thing around my neck. Last time the end of the fag fell off into the lampshade and burnt my throat," Butty replied.

"Fair enough kidda. The last thing we want is the smell of your skin burning. I mean, what's the point in dressing up as Sir Spamalot of Castle Crazy if you're going to smell like a human BBQ?" Dave replied with a wry smile.

"You're a funny fucker Dave, has anyone ever told you that?" Butty replied.

"All the fucking time Butty lad. Listen, I'm only messing you know that right? I only take the piss out of people I like and I've already told you I think you're a good egg. I'm glad you're John's brother. Fuck knows what we would have done last night if it wasn't for you. John has told me a lot about you over the years and I know you're not a people person so opening up your home and letting me stay can't have been easy. What you've done with your house is superb. Mental but superb and I'm glad you're around. I take the piss a lot but it's only banter. It's the only way I know how to deal with all the horrible shit that's happening so don't take offence," Dave said.

"None taken Dave. How can I be offended by a man that looks like he's stepped out of a Prefab Sprout video and walks around carrying a giant spoon?" came Butty's response.

"Touché Butty lad touché! We best get moving. I've got four tabs left and if you think I'm a sarcastic twat now you don't want to see me without any smokes. Point the way then lad and I'll make the journey enjoyable by telling you why back in the 80s, having a movie with the title song written and performed by Kenny Loggins guaranteed you a box office smash!" Dave replied.

They pulled away from the house with Butty directing them to the small row of shops on Russell Road. It was a quick and uneventful journey with only a scattering of zombies on the streets that paid no attention to the moving Thunderbird.

Dave brought the car to a halt 100 yards away from their destination. A blue van parked outside the shops sent alarm bells ringing in his head and he thought it best to keep a safe distance. It wasn't that the van looked out of place that worried them but the fact it was shaking from side to side.

"What do you reckon?" Dave asked.

Butty reached inside his lampshade neck protector and pulled out a pair of large binoculars, giving him a closer view of the van.

"Could be zombies? Maybe even people being held captive?" he replied.

"Let's have a proper look then kidda," Dave said, reaching for the binoculars.

Instead of handing them over, Butty again reached inside his lampshade neck protector and retrieved another set of binoculars, passing them to Dave.

"Cor blimey, you're like an apocalyptic Mary Poppins! How much stuff have you got in there? Have a dig around and see if you've got Freedom of Choice by Devo. Classic album that lar and a great band too. In fact, you look like you could be in Devo wearing that clobber. All you need is a plant pot on your head and you could start a tribute act," said Dave.

Butty didn't reply, instead he reached inside his neck protector then pulled out his hand, presenting Dave with his middle finger.

They gave the van a closer inspection, watching as it continued to shake violently. Then suddenly it stopped and the side door opened. Out stepped a small thin man with a bald head and terrible skin condition. He paced back and forth for several minutes muttering to himself, stopping only to boot the van occasionally. Finally he appeared to calm down, leaning against the vehicle and lighting a cigarette. Dave took a closer look into the van through its open side door. There he saw hundreds of cartons of cigarettes as well as copious amounts of booze, food and medical supplies.

"Any thoughts Ace?" Dave asked.

"It's unlikely he's on his own. The others are probably in the shop adding to their stash. Let's just sit here a while and watch. If he is on his own then maybe we could reason with him. Maybe make a trade. We've got a duffle bag full of weapons in the boot, we could try to reach an agreement." Butty replied

For a while they watched as the man finished his cigarette, booted the van again then climbed back inside, closing the side door. No other activity followed and Dave was quickly becoming impatient.

"We've got to check it out Ace and maybe make a trade like you said. I mean look how much stuff there is. Even if we only come away with a fraction of what's in that van it would still set us up for a while," Dave said.

"Agreed but let's approach with caution and keep an eye on the shops. If we see he has other survivors with him then we leave. Zombies are one thing but dealing with the living is something else," Butty replied.

Leaving the vehicle, Butty retrieved one of the large duffle bags from the boot and they slowly moved forward - Dave, with Battle Paddle in hand, doing so purposely and Butty because his jeans were too tight. The road was quiet with only a scattering of zombies on the street and they treated Dave and Butty like they didn't exist. Instead they sniffed the air keenly, following their nose.

Dave arrived at the van first and looked to Butty, motioning for him to hurry up. Butty, moving as fast as he could, whispered to Dave, telling him to wait before alerting the man inside to their presence. Dave misheard and thought Butty had given him the go ahead and so whacked the Battle Paddle against the van.

"Knock knock Kidda. Swap you a crowbar for a carton of ciggies," he shouted.

Quickly and without warning the side door of the van opened and the man inside jumped out, brandishing a knife, thrusting it towards Dave. Luckily for Dave, the man caught his foot against a crate of beer and he slipped from the van, landing hard in the road, cracking his forehead against the cold tarmac.

"Fuck me Ace did you hear his head crack against the floor? If he's not dead then Gary Numan isn't the greatest musician of all time!" Dave declared.

"He's not dead," Butty informed, checking their attacker.

"Isn't he? Well then forget everything I just said," Dave replied.

Blood trickled from the man's scabby head, the fall knocking him unconscious.

"It's his own fault. What was the crazy bastard thinking? Leaping out at me like that," Dave said, filling his pockets with cigarettes from inside the van.

"He must have got his foot caught when he jumped," Butty replied, "I can't see any activity from the shops. Let's take what we can and get out of here. It's his own fault for attacking us. Maybe when he comes to it'll teach him a lesson."

"Already on it Ace, let's load the car and scarper," Dave said, a mountain of cigarette cartons in his arms.

Journal Entry 12

"I spy with my little eye, something beginning with... err...err... S."

"Spam!"

"Correct!"

"Ok, my turn. I spy with my little eye, something beginning with... erm.. dododoo... err... S."

"Spam!"

It was the worst game of I Spy I had ever played and believe me when I tell you I have played some whoppers over the years with my brother. To this day he still thinks you spell cushion with a 'K' and we grew up in a house with a lot of 'Kushions'.

Dave and Butty had been gone for some time and with the outside of the house secured, we were drastically running out of things to do to keep ourselves busy. Before the apocalypse it was easy. You could watch TV, listen to music, surf the net, read a book or just enjoy a little quiet time. Trust me when I tell you that quiet time is not something you want when all your friends are dead or undead. The last thing you want is time to reflect on all that has happened. I would go crazy if I took time out to think about all the terrible acts I have committed. The best thing to do is to keep busy and unfortunately for Emily,

Jonathon and I, all we could think of was a game of I Spy. Not the best game when you are sat in a room that pretty much only contains Spam.

Finally, the rumbling engine of the Thunderbird could be heard pulling up outside, followed by the doors slamming as my brother and Dave left the vehicle.

"Ace! Drop the ladder from Butty's bedroom. The shitty rope ladder won't cut it," I heard Dave yell from outside.

Man it was good to hear his voice. We rushed into my brother's room, removed the wooden planks from the window and I looked down into the garden to see Dave with about ten lit cigarettes in his mouth and a crate of bottled lager under each arm, his face projecting a smile bigger than the dump he left floating in the toilet earlier.

"Miss me?" he smiled.

"Like a hole in the head," I replied, lowering the retractable ladder from the open window.

"Hey there's no need for that lar. We come bearing gifts. We've got booze, fags, food, medical supplies, magazines and books. Everything you could possibly need to make the apocalypse an enjoyable experience," he said.

"Dave, as surprised as I am with your bounty, I am more astounded that you can talk at all never mind deliver a perfectly audible sentence with a load of fags hanging out of your gob," I said.

"Ah well, you see, only real dedicated smokers can pull this off. It's one of the many things than make me a cool bastard. Talking of cool bastards, Butty should be here in a minute. I have to hand it to him, he knows what he's doing when it comes to zombies lar that's for sure. Here he is now. Oi! C3-PO, come and tell your John what you did," Dave said.

Walking into view came Butty in full combat gear minus his lamp shade neck protector. He was carrying a bumper pack of toilet roll under one arm and a large collection of magazines, the only one of which I could make out was a men's magazine called FHM, famous for its scantily clad buxom models.

"I see you've got your night planned out then brother?" I said.

"Eh? Oh right, a masturbation joke. Very funny. I bet you're really proud of that one." Butty replied.

I was actually.

"If you can pull your mind out of the gutter, I'll explain why we have these magazines. There are two reasons. Firstly, we lived in a world swamped with information. Everywhere we looked there were TV shows, movies, radio stations, music, Facebook, Twitter, Xboxes, PlayStations, Nintendo, applications, Angry fucking Birds... Every conceivable way of bombarding people with ways to keep their minds distracted. That's all gone now so we're back to basics. Reading and talking to each other. Secondly, if you secure these magazines around your legs and arms with tape they could save your life. There isn't a zombie around that can chomp through an issue of Cosmopolitan quicker than I can ram a knife through its skull. Anyway, more survival tips when we get inside. Make yourself useful and give us a hand shifting this lot, there's more in the car," he instructed.

Forty minutes later and we were all stood in Butty's room. Emily, Jonathon and I were in awe at the bounty before us; Dave and my brother displayed grins like Cheshire Cats. There were cans and bottled lager, whisky and vodka, bread, fresh (ish) meat, soft drinks, chocolate, crisps, pizzas and for reasons I couldn't quite figure, about forty tins of corned beef.

"What's with all the corned beef? Finally had enough of spam?" I asked Butty who had already made a start on the lager.

"It's everything we could take from the van," he replied, followed by the loudest burp the apocalypse had ever heard, "Sorry about that. Gassy lager."

Butty and Dave went on to explain how they had intended to ransack the newsagents on Russell Road but when they arrived someone was already inside and their van had been left open. So whilst the owners were looting the shop, Butty and Dave swooped in and stole the stash from the van, transferring over as much as they could to the Thunderbird before buggering off back home. They made it sound so simple but my brother's poker face was awful. I can always tell when he's lying as he looks like he needs to take a shit.

"As simple as that was it? You just waltzed up to the van and stole their gear without them noticing and then you came straight back here? Pull the other one, Russell Road is only 5 minutes away and you've been gone for a lot longer than that. Come on, out with it. What really happened?" I asked.

"Pretty much what Butty said Ace, give or take a few minor details," Dave replied, sparking a cigarette and also helping himself to a beer.

"Come on Uncle Butty what really happened? I bet Russell Road was really filled with zombies and you and Dave had to fight your way to the shop, slaying hundreds of walkers just so we could eat pizza and you could have your smokes. Is that what really happened?" Emily asked excitedly.

"I bet Emily's right. How did you kill them all? With the Battle Paddle? Crow bar? Stomping on their heads with your boots or did you use your bare hands?" Jonathon asked, almost as enthusiastic as Emily.

I looked Butty and Dave up and down. They didn't have any zombie splatter on them and looked as fresh as they did before they left. Whatever happened, zombies were not involved and I could see Butty's terrible poker face wavering under pressure from the Runcorn Gestapo.

"Butty if you don't tell me the truth, I will tell everyone about that time when we were kids and I caught you in

Granddad's shed with our next door neighbour's bra, Vaseline and a cheese grater," I threatened.

That did the trick!

"Alright you bunch of bastards. If you must know then I'll tell you..." Butty started.

The minor details that Butty had omitted were that when they had approached the blue van a man jumped out of the vehicle attempting to protect his loot but he had done so clumsily, falling heavily to the floor, cracking his head and knocking himself out. Butty and Dave derived from the botched attack that the man was trouble and instead of helping him, they took as much of the loot as they could and left him lying in the road with blood gushing from his head.

I would be lying if I said this didn't worry me. Not because they had left a man dying in the road. We have just as much to fear from the living as we do from the dead and the way they had described him he wasn't exactly friendly. What worried me was this man's companions, the ones that Butty said were inside the newsagents. Had they seen what had happened? If they did then would they hold Butty and Dave responsible for what happened to their friend?

"Don't worry Ace, we were like lightning. In and out in no time. I doubt anyone saw what happened. It's not like they would be able to track us down if they did. Runcorn is a big place kidda, made even bigger by the dead twats roaming around. Even if they did come looking for us this place is pretty secure. Just look at the size of the overgrowth outside. And with all the stakes you've hammered into the ground... You would have to be wacko to attempt anything, especially now it's getting dark outside. We'll be fine lar now grab yourself a beer and I'll cook up a few of these pizzas. We've had a shit couple of days, it'll do us all good to unwind a little," Dave said.

Dave was a man that took everything in his stride, even the zombie apocalypse. I was often surprised at how little things fazed him and I had found his outlook calming. Although I still held concerns, it was clear that Dave and Butty were not worried so I was prepared to put it to the back of my mind, crack open a beer and do as instructed and unwind or try to at least. We had been through a lot and an evening relaxing with my family and best friend sounded perfect.

"Whilst Dave sorts out the grub I'm going to do a final perimeter check, just to be on the safe side. I won't be long and I might have a little surprise for you all when I get back," Butty said leaving the room.

Emily and Jonathon had already opened some of the chocolate and I could see them eyeing up the booze but daring not to take any.

"Now then love birds. At fifteen years old you are both well under the legal drinking age. But those rules belong to another time. Things are different now and by my reckoning fifteen in apocalypse years makes you... oooh twenty one I'd say. But go easy, don't be taking advantage of my good nature," I said.

"Thanks Dad, you're the best!" Emily said flinging her arms around me.

"Yeah thanks Mr Diant, I mean John," Jonathon said reaching for a bottle of whisky then changing his mind and opting for a beer after seeing the stern "Don't you fucking dare!" look on my face.

I may not win father of the year but with any luck, a little beer buzz will help cloud Emily and Jonathon's mind sufficiently enough so they forget the horror of the last few days. At least for a little while anyway. I was hoping for the same and the first few beers were some of the best I had ever tasted. The cold golden nectar felt amazing as it passed through my mouth, coating my throat then spreading a warm fuzzy feeling through my body. The beer was doing its job superbly and I was pleasantly relaxed. That was until Butty reappeared with bottles of his cheese beer. I don't really remember anything after that!

Revenge

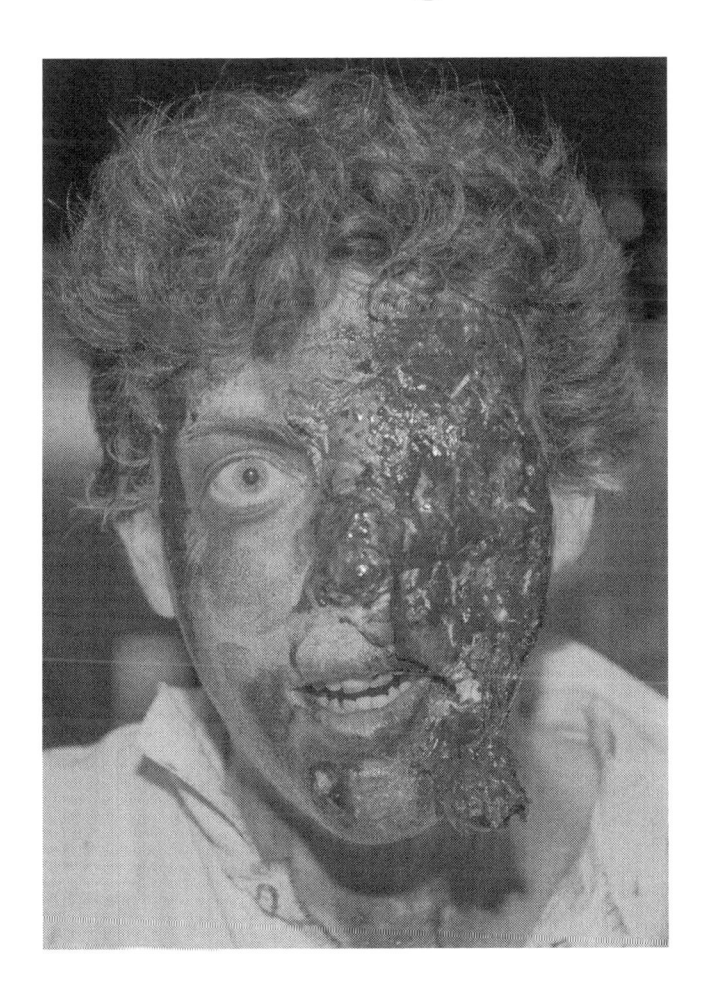

Ged flicked ash onto the thick shag pile carpet that covered the apartment floor. Yesterday felt so far away and his previous life as a notorious loan shark a distant memory. Peering through the window, he took a long pull on his cigarette, wincing as the inhaled smoke burnt through his throat. Ged Woods was not a heavy smoker but he had found himself sucking down cigarette after cigarette for the past few hours. Not through the stress brought on by the zombie apocalypse, the loss of his home or the knowledge that almost everyone he had ever known was now dead. He couldn't care less. But instead to mask the smell of the quickly decaying elderly woman he had viciously murdered the night before when himself, his cousin Joni and his three employees, Tom, Ed and Andy, took the apartment for themselves. His employees had felt the death of the old lady was unnecessary but had not spoken out. Knowing their volatile employer as well as they did, they thought it best to stay quiet and fall in line. They valued their lives too much to cross the boss and didn't want to suffer the same fate as the poor elderly lady.

Joni became extremely animated following Ged's killing of the old lady and watched in delight as his cousin wrapped his hands around her thin frail neck and squeezed the life out of her. Then, to make sure she would not return as a zombie, he took a knitting needle that had been resting next to a ball of wool in her lap and stabbed her through the forehead. Joni was so engrossed in the kill, that he had stood behind his cousin and mimicked his every movement, placing his dry flaking hands around an invisible neck as he felt the rush of the kill. Then he stabbed an invisible knitting needle through an invisible forehead. Filled with bloodlust, he had not wanted Ged to stop, begging his cousin to hang her dead body from the window to display her murdered corpse to any survivors thinking of taking the apartment for themselves. Knowing how excitable Joni can be, Ged calmly refused his suggestion, stating that the first person to try and take the apartment would be his to kill and to do with as he pleased. This eased his psychotic desires.

Joni was an exception to Ged's rules. Being family he felt self-assured in his cousin's presence and was cocksure with his behaviour towards the others. Joni was a small man with a terrible skin condition. It was dry and would crack and itch constantly. This caused flaking and puss filled sores to cover his head, face and neck. Because of his condition, he continually scratted at his skin and would leave a trail of flaky flesh everywhere he went. Despite his physical appearance he was always acting the big man and revelled in talking down to Tom and Ed. Especially Tom, who was often the victim of verbal attacks from this weasel of a man. Be it Tom's size or his intelligence, Joni was relentless with his insults and mocking. This bully boy behaviour did not sit well with Ed who liked to think of himself as an older brother to his friend. He felt protective of Tom and saw it as his duty to keep him away from trouble. Without Ed's calming influence Tom may well have lost control and lashed out, ending the insults permanently. Ed had often fantasised of what would happen come the day when Ged was no longer a concern and he could let Tom loose on Joni. Every outcome for this scenario played out the same. It ended with Joni's death. Fantasies would have to suffice for the time being though because in reality there was nothing Ed could do to stop

Joni's persistent petulant behaviour. He was the boss' cousin and, despite his annoyances, Ged valued Joni above all others and would not have a bad word said against him.

When not in his cousin's presence, Joni wasn't so arrogant. He would turn to whining with threats of telling Ged if anyone mistreated him. Knowing the dislike the others held for him he dared not berate as he would if his cousin was there.

The only person other than Ged that favoured Joni was Andy but this had been a recent development and he had only done so to stay in the boss' good books. Ged liked his staff to be obedient, to not ask questions, be punctual, to do exactly as instructed and, most importantly, to be loyal. If you worked for him, you worked for no other and that included any side businesses you ran privately. Andy had been dealing in stolen vehicles without informing his boss, knowing very well that he would be made to stop immediately. What's more, he had been acquiring the stolen vehicles during the hours he was meant to be working for his employer. It had not taken long for Ged to realise what was happening and he had summoned Andy to his home to confront him and establish where his loyalty lay. You were given one chance to redeem yourself if you worked for Ged and this was Andy's.

It was Joni that delivered the message and had the responsibility of escorting Andy to Ged's home. Andy had known instantly what it was about and he was petrified. His greed and lies had not, as he had hoped, gone unnoticed and now he had to answer to the boss and at his home too. Almost nobody who went to the boss' house was seen again. Ever.

The zombie apocalypse hit Runcorn as Joni was taking him to see Ged and they were involved in a car crash, swerving to avoid a small horde of zombies that were ripping a police man limb from limb in the road ahead. Joni found himself trapped in the wreckage. With his seat belt jammed, he was strapped tightly to the driver's seat. Andy had a difficult decision to make. Leave Joni and run, run and try to make his way on his own, or save his boss's cousin and take him to Ged thus proving his loyalty and value. He chose the latter, returning home with Joni first to retrieve his trusted and beloved blue 55 plate Citroen Relay transit van. With all hell breaking loose, he figured he would stand a better chance with Ged and his men than he would on his own – a choice that would ultimately lead to his death.

They arrived at Ged's home to find it on fire, with Ged stood on his garage roof, surrounded by flames, manically throwing petrol bombs at the encroaching zombies. Now instead of just walking corpses wanting to eat him, they were also walking fire balls. With minutes to spare he jumped from his garage, landing on top of Andy's van. They then sped to the Dockside Pub on Sandy Lane, their regular meeting place. There they found Tom and Ed surrounded by the undead, desperately defending themselves, using pool cues and broken beer pumps as weapons. If they had not arrived when they did, both Ed and Tom would surely have died.

Allowing the smoke to seep out of his mouth and engulf his face, Ged looked upon his reflection in the apartment window. It appeared distorted in the thick nicotine smoke. He noted his image was not unlike that of the undead that in their droves were shuffling past his window. For several hours he had watched as more and more zombies passed by, slowly walking by the apartment. At first he hid himself from view, nervous that if they saw him he would draw their attention. As the minutes then hours ticked over he became daring, gradually showing himself to the zombies more and more until finally standing in full view, watching in disbelief as they ignored him and instead slowly lumbered along the road, heading to the same place - The Pavilions.

After a time, he started to feel offended by the lack of interest shown towards him and even went as far as yelling and banging on the window but still they shuffled past. It was lonely trying to make the undead want to eat you. Why were they not showing an interest? At first he could not figure this out but then, whilst searching for a transmission using his elderly victim's radio, he tuned into the Halton Community Radio emergency transmission, informing survivors to make their way to the Pavilions if they needed shelter. Everything fell into place. The lure of so much living flesh in one place was too much for the undead to ignore and they must somehow have sensed their presence. Why show interest in a pitiful singular snack when there was an all you can eat human buffet down the road?

"Have you seen this?" he said to the dead elderly lady in the chair, "Nah of course you haven't what am I thinking? That knitting needle is obstructing your view."

Ged approached the woman and pulled the knitting needle from her forehead forcefully. Blood few from her wound as the needle was removed and sprayed across the window.

"Now look what you've done. Well that's going to have to be cleaned isn't it? No it's fine, don't get up, you stay where you are, I'll do it. What was that? Yes I know I'm talking to a dead person but I've been on my own all day with nothing to do but smoke cigarettes and scream at zombies. Lesson learnt I guess. I'll get one of the minions to hold the fort next time and I'll go out killing zombies and looting shops. It beats being stuck here talking to you. No offense, dear, but you're not exactly the life and soul of the party now are you?"

The sound of Andy's van could be heard screeching to a halt outside the apartment. Ged looked through the window in time to see it pull up and smash into several of the undead. The van then backed up, pushing its rear against the door to the apartment.

"Finally!" he said, moving away from the window, rushing to the apartment door.

"Now Tom remember what I told you. You just stay quiet and let me do all the talking and if Ged does speak to you, what do you say?" Ed asked of his nervous friend.

"I just, I just say there was two men. There was two men and I say nothing else. I won't say a word, Ed, I promise, I promise I won't," Tom jittered, nervously fidgeting with a tin of corned beef.

"That's good Tom, remember that and leave the rest to me. Everything will be ok, there's no need to be nervous. I got this," Ed reassured, leaving the driver's seat and clambering into the back of the van.

He took a deep breath, composed himself then opened the rear van doors. Waiting in the apartment doorway was Ged, eager to inspect the bounty that had taken his men all day to scavenge.

"And where have you fuckers been all day? I sent you out for supplies, not to find the Lost Cities of Gold!" Ged complained, not yet realising Joni and Andy's absence.

"We ran into a few unexpected problems," Ed said solemnly.

It was Ed's response or more so the delivery of it that grabbed Ged's attention. He looked into the van, past Ed and to Tom, who was slumped in the passenger seat, sniffling with fear whilst stuffing his face with corned beef. A fire started to burn deep within him and his vision blurred with rage.

"WHERE IS HE? WHERE'S JONI?" Ged yelled with spittle flying from his mouth and his face shaking in anger.

"Andy was…" Ed started.

"FUCK ANDY, WHERE'S MY COUSIN?" Ged growled.

Ed took a breath. He had not anticipated being interrupted and needed to quickly compose himself before restarting his story.

"We were ambushed by two men, heavily armoured. Tom and I were inside the newsagents on Russell Road whilst Joni was guarding the van. They shot him then took the loot. I'm sorry Ged, he's dead. There was nothing we could do. If we'd have left the shop then we'd be dead to!" a nervous Ed explained.

Consumed by anger, Ged jumped up into the van and grabbed Ed's throat, pushing him against the floor of the transit.

"I… I know… know what they… look like. We can find them…" Ed choked.

"One had a lamp shade around his neck and was wearing really tight pants. The other had sunglasses on and was holding a giant spoon. They had a really old car too," Tom said quickly before returning to shovelling food into his mouth.

Tom's description forced Ged to loosen his grip on Ed's neck and his rage subsided enough for his mind to process a structured thought. If these men were as distinguishable as Tom had described, then maybe they could track them down. Their death would be much more satisfying than Ed's.

He retracted his hands from Ed's neck.

"Take me to Joni, I want to see him," Ged demanded.

Ged said nothing during the short journey from Sandy Lane to Russell Road. Instead he sat, stony faced, staring straight ahead whilst Tom whimpered and Ed drove, informing his boss of the truth regarding Andy's demise and the lies about Joni's killing.

It was a strained ride and Ed's heart beat faster the closer they got to where Joni was left. He just hoped that the zombies had eaten enough of him so Ged would buy his bullshit story. If not, then the lack of a gunshot wound was going to be difficult to explain.

As the shops became visible so did Joni's body, or what was left of it. Two Zombies knelt next to him, devouring what remained of his corpse. Before Ed could bring the van to a stop, Ged climbed over Tom and opened the door, pushing the big man out of the way then jumping from the moving vehicle. He tumbled onto the road before quickly pulling himself to his feet, running at the zombies whilst screaming like a man possessed.

He grabbed the first of the undead by its hair, pulling it away from the remains of Joni. Forcefully he rammed the zombie's head into the road over and over until its skull cracked and grey rotting brains spilled on to the cold tarmac. Moving to the other zombie he swung a well-placed kick to its face, sending it flying backwards. Lost in a rage he dove on top of it, laying punch after punch into its face, breaking first the nose, then the jaw, then its eyes became bloodied and slowly the thin dead face of the zombie started to break apart until like the first, it was no more.

With the zombies now destroyed he rose to his feet and let out an almighty scream. Part in anger and part in triumph. He looked down upon what remained of his cousin. The dead had devoured almost every inch of his body, leaving only his open sore and puss covered head intact.

It would appear even zombies had limits.

Ed, followed by a nervous and cowering Tom, joined their boss to look over the remains of Joni. "This is perfect," Ed thought to himself. The zombies had done him a favour and there was no way Ged could tell if his cousin had been shot or not. Any pot holes in his lies had now been covered. If he played this right both he and Tom would be safe and closer than ever to their boss who, with Joni gone, had nobody else to rely on.

"This is the exact spot where they shot him. The van was parked here and the guy with the lamp shade around his neck was over there. It was him that pulled the trigger but not at first. At first he gave Joni the chance to run but he refused. I watched discreetly from the shop window as he stood his ground and tried to rush the guy with the gun.

He knew what he was doing, boss. He could have easily run away and given me and Tom up but he didn't. He knew that if he was to do that then we would all be dead. He gave his life so that we could live. The other guy, the one wearing sunglasses, looted the van and loaded up their vehicle, the old 80s Thunderbird I told you about. They filled that car with as much of our stash as they could. Then they drove away, heading towards Weston Road. Once they had gone, Tom and I left the shop and hurried to help Joni but it was too late boss, he was already dead. The noise of the gun shot had alerted a few zombies to our location so we decided to get the hell out of there and we drove straight to you," Ed explained nervously.

"And these men, they were dressed funny?" Ged asked without taking his eyes from the head of his dead cousin.

"That's right Boss they, they were dressed real strange," Tom informed, grasping his chance to confirm the only bit of truth in Ed's story.

"What are you thinking boss? These are dangerous men," Ed said.

"I am a dangerous man! Now Joni has been taken from me I have nothing to lose and there is nothing more dangerous than a man with nothing to lose!" Ged scowled.

He placed his right foot over the torn remains of Joni's neck and pulled his head free, taking it in his hands. He then lifted the head so it was face to face with his own.

"What was that Joni? Yes I agree. Men like that can't be too hard to find. Go after them you say? Make them pay for what they did to you? Well if you insist Cousin, if you insist," Ged snarled, offering a menacing stare along Russell Road in the direction Ed had said Joni's killers had driven.

"He does know Joni is dead doesn't he?" Tom whispered in Ed's ear.

Ed shushed Tom, placing a hand gently over his mouth. Luckily for them both, Ged had not heard a thing and was deep in thought, formulating their next move.

Ged, with Joni's head in hand, turned quickly and marched back to the van, signalling for Ed and Tom to follow. He opened the rear van doors and inspected the content. Amongst the remaining bottles of booze and tinned food stuffs he found a rucksack full with the deceased Andy's clothes. He emptied the rucksack, littered the road with the content then, finding an old rag, he wiped Joni's head in an attempt to remove the blood and puss that covered the scabby pale skin. This did little to reduce the gloop that coated his cousin's head, serving only as a way of smearing it more. Ged was satisfied though and he placed Joni's head inside the rucksack and slung it over his shoulder. Turning his attention back to the content of the van he inspected a large metal cage containing blankets and a chewed plastic steak toy.

"Andy would put his dog in that whenever he needed to take him anywhere," Ed informed.

"Thank you Mr Andy Deen!" Ged said with an evil smile, "Who would have thought that the only time he would be of any use to me was when he was dead? I have plans for that cage. Come with me."

Ed and Tom followed their boss as he marched towards a pair of shuffling zombies that were heading in the direction of Sandy Lane and ultimately, The Pavilions.

"Here zombies, zombies, lots of lovely flesh for you, come on, come on now, follow me for a tasty snack!" he said, attempting to lure the undead back to the van but they showed little interest, sniffing at him briefly but preferring to continue their journey rather than take the bait.

"It's the bag, it's masking your scent, they can smell Joni. They won't come near you whilst you're carrying his head." Ed said, the words struggling to leave his mouth.

Ged removed the rucksack from his shoulder and tossed the bag over to Ed who caught it then instantly puked as he felt Joni's head below the fabric. His boss offered a disapproving look, as if nausea was a sign of weakness, so he lowered his head apologetically but he didn't mean it. After all he had never handled a corpse's head before, let alone one as disgusting as Joni's.

Now free of his cousin's rotting head, Ged tried again to get the undead's attention. This time they paid more of an interest in him but the lure of The Pavilions was still too much for them to ignore.

"Argh! What the fuck does a man need to do to make a zombie want to eat you in this town?" he screamed before removing his jacket and biting deeply into his own arm.

With blood dripping from the fresh wound he pushed his arm in front of the zombie's faces. This did the trick and they finally took the bait, following Ged to the van.

Ed jumped into the van and opened the cage doors before exiting again. Ged was next to climb inside followed closely by his two hungry suitors. Once in the van, Ed climbed in behind and pushed them both into the cage, locking its door quickly.

"Now we need to find the men that killed Joni and I'll search every house in every street if I have to. Let's go, head towards Weston Road, there can't be many Ford Thunderbirds on the roads," Ged said.

They drove away, covering most of the estate before moving onto Weston Road. They only saw the dead, both shuffling and torn apart. The van's suspension was thoroughly tested as it bounced over body after body. The once smooth tarmac now felt like off road driving under the ageing frame of the Citroen transit. Ed was thankful when they moved onto Weston Road and the dead became sparse, only the many feathered corpses remained. It was then, in the lessoning daylight, Ged spotted the Ford Thunderbird parked up ahead. He motioned for Ed to bring the van to a halt and he sat, silently staring at the vehicle for several minutes.

Ed was nervous. He had not expected they would come across the vehicle so soon. In fact, he was hoping they would not find it at all. He questioned how far he was willing to go to protect his and Tom's life. Could he see his lie through knowing all too well what the consequences could be? What Ged was capable of? He had to, he had no choice. If the boss was to discover the truth about Joni, that his death was due to his own stupidity and clumsiness, he would definitely lay blame with Tom and him. No, he had to see this through, no matter the cost. Tom was as good as a brother and he would do anything to protect him.

"Wait in the van, me and Joni have got this," Ged said, exiting the vehicle with his cousin's head in the rucksack.

Whilst Ged slowly moved towards the Ford Thunderbird, Tom broke down, unable to contain his upset any longer.

"We've done bad Ed, we've done a bad thing. Now Ged is going to kill those guys and they didn't do anything. They didn't do what we said they did. They are gonna die because we told lies!" Tom cried.

"Hey, hey, Tom it's OK. Yes we told a lie but those guys are not entirely innocent. It's true they didn't kill Joni but they did take all of our stuff. They took our drinks, our smokes and they took our food. That was your food too. We made a great sacrifice to get that loot. You remember what happened to Andy don't you? We deserve that loot, not them. If Joni hadn't been so stupid and knocked himself out then maybe we would still have it. You know what? I bet that's all Ged is doing. I bet he's going to see where they stashed our stuff so we can take it back. I bet nobody has to get hurt at all," said Ed, trying to ease Tom's concern.

"Ed, he was talking to Joni's head like he was still alive. He's gone cuckoo. He's not all there. If he sees those guys there's no telling what he could do. I don't want to be part of killing no-one. With the bad men it's different but with normal people, people like us? I can't do that Ed, I can't, I can't, I can't…" Tom again cried.

Ed put his arm around his friend to comfort him. Tom's large frame meant it barely reached past the big guy's shoulder. Seeing his friend so upset was difficult and again he questioned if he had done the right thing. "Too late to turn back now" he thought to himself, watching as Ged approached the Ford Thunderbird.

Ged slowly walked alongside the Ford Thunderbird, running his hand against the cold body of the vehicle. He tried every door handle. Locked. On the floor in front of the driver's seat he saw a cassette tape snapped in two, "The greatest hits of Curtis Steiger" and ejected from the cassette player was "Dare" by the Human League. He surmised from this that the car did not originally belong to its current owners and that, like the loot in the van, they had taken this car for themselves, probably killing the original owner in doing so. His thinking was that the broken Curtis Steiger tape belonged to the original owner and had been broken and replaced with the Human League by one of the thieves that took it. He was right, but not in the way he imagined.

On the front passenger seat rested a modified lamp shade. He remembered what Ed had told him and how he described the attire of the man that pulled the trigger and shot Joni.

"The van was parked here and the guy with the lamp shade around his neck was over there. It was him that pulled the trigger…" he recalled.

He was now in no doubt that this was the vehicle they had been searching for and he reasoned that his cousin's killers were probably residing in a house close by but which one? It didn't take him long to find out. The smell of decaying flesh first drew him to the large detached house, hidden behind thick overgrowth. He looked back to Ed and Tom who were watching from inside the van and he offered them an evil smile, pulled out a flick knife and stabbed every tyre of the Thunderbird then motioned for them to come over. He did not wait for them before investigating further, he was too eager to see the faces of the men responsible for his pain.

"I wanna stay in the van Ed. Please don't make me go with Ged. He's gone cuckoo and has evil in his eyes. More evil than the bad men that are everywhere. He's gonna do something bad I just know it and I don't want any part of it," Tom blubbed, tears running down his chubby food stained cheeks.

"Believe me, if you stay here in the van and go against Ged, you'll see how evil he is. Just keep close to me and here, take these," Ed said, handing Tom a hand full of chocolate bars and a tin of corned beef, "when you feel yourself getting upset or afraid, just eat. It will make you better OK?"

Ed had barely given his advice when Tom was almost finished with his second bar of chocolate. So he reached into the glove compartment and retrieved another 3 chocolate bars, handing them to his friend.

They both exited the van and quickly moved towards the Thunderbird. When they got there Ged was nowhere to be seen but to their right in the stone wall that ran along the pavement of the Road, they saw an open gate, leading down into thick overgrowth. They carefully took to the steps, Ed first with Tom following closely. It was a treacherous climb, made difficult by the dusk sky and the thick branches and brambles obscuring the steps below their feet.

Ed walked with his arms stretched forward, pushing the overgrowth to the sides. At one point he felt his hand touch the tip of a sharp wooden spike. The people that lived here had taken steps to keep unwanted guests out. He gulped and took a long breath to steady his nerves. What other traps lay in waiting he wondered.

Finally they reached the bottom of the steps, walking out into an open clearing. There stood Ged, inspecting a row of 5 frost covered decapitated zombie heads on spikes, protecting a doorway to a large detached house completely covered in limbs.

"Beautiful, absolutely stunning. You know, if I didn't need to hurt these guys I think we could have been friends. I mean just look at what they've done with this place. And the smell! No zombie would look at this place twice. Inspiring," Ged whispered.

Tom did not share Ged's view of the property's external décor and the combination of fear mixed with the terrible smell of rotting flesh and the large amount of chocolate he had guzzled resulted in brown, acidy chunks of part digested confectionery projecting from his mouth.

"I'm, I'm sorry but it's the smell, I can't help it," Tom spluttered then vomited again, "Make the smell go away!"

"Ed shut him up will you?" Ged demanded.

Ed fumbled around in his pockets whilst Tom continued to vomit, his retching getting louder with each hurl. Finally he found what he was looking for, a packet of mints. Opening them he took two of the mints and quickly shoved them up Tom's nose and he collapsed to the floor, breathing in deeply through his nose then out through his mouth over and over. The cool minty freshness blocked the rancid stink of the undead and quickly he calmed down and his stomach stopped churning.

"Are you OK now?" Ed asked of his friend.

"Uh huh" Tom replied. He would have said yes but he had already shoved another chocolate bar in his mouth and Ed had always told him to never speak with his mouth full.

Hearing a noise from inside the house, Ged signalled for Ed and Tom to be quiet. Looking to the boarded up window above he heard laughter and a loud Scouse voice bellowed...

"Beer made with cheese? Fuck that lar, I'd rather drink my own piss and that smells like beef noodles so God only knows what it tastes like..."

Laughter again could be heard from inside and Ged surmised that there was definitely more than two people in the house such was the fullness and mixed tone of the merriment. He looked to Ed and smiled again. Now he knew there were more of them, the game was on and he was revelling in the challenge of making these people pay for Joni's death. But first he had to find a way in without arousing suspicion.

Ged, followed closely by Ed and Tom, moved from the front of the house and quietly they made their way to the back, using the external side wall of the house as a guide. The putrid smell of decaying bodies intensified with every step and sensing that Tom was again about to hurl, Ed shoved another two polo mints up the big guy's nostrils.

Ged was the first to turn the corner, entering the large back garden. His eyes widened in amazement at the sight of the deathly heap of slayed zombies that greeted him. Ed was not so much amazed but petrified. What had his lies taken them to?

"There must be over a hundred corpses. It would have taken more than two people to kill this many. I think we should put the brakes on and plan exactly what it is you want to do before we go any further. Who knows how many are inside," Ed said, trying to talk Ged out of doing something that could get them all killed.

"Maybe it took more than two or maybe the two were just very organised. Are you saying that we couldn't do the same? With my brains, Tom's strength and your… erm… ability to follow orders, we could build a mountain of zombies bigger than this, no problem. The whole purpose of this is to mask their scent and to scare people away. Just look at you, you're petrified! For God's sake man, pull yourself together. I don't care how many are inside that house. There could be a small army for all I care but one way or another I'm going inside and I will make them pay for what they did. Now help me find a way in," Ged demanded.

Ed swallowed his fear and helped Ged look for a way inside, pulling on the handle of the locked rear door. Every window had been boarded shut. Without tools and the use of force, there appeared to be no way of gaining entry. Then he heard a large wooden crack followed by glass shattering.

"Oops," Tom said, his right foot pushed through a broken wooden plank covering a window in the floor at the base of the house.

"Tom if you weren't so fat and ugly I could kiss you. You've just found our way in!" Ged said excitedly.

Tom in his clumsiness had stepped through a wooden board nailed over a small narrow window belonging to the cellar of the house. Neither Ed nor Tom were small enough to fit through such a small gap but Ged, despite his strength and stature, was a slight man and would fit through easily.

Without hesitation, he pulled the broken wood from the broken window and slid himself through the opening, leaving the rucksack containing Joni's head outside. Inside the cellar it was dark, the only light provided coming from the twilight sky shining through the window. He strained his eyes in an effort to adjust quickly to the change but it was so dark he could only make out shapes. Two large objects were to his immediate left. He touched their cool metal exterior and his nose filled with the strong smell of petrol. He wasn't sure but he guessed by their size and feel that they were generators.

Feeling his way around the cellar, he moved forward till his foot pushed into a large stack of something, bringing it clattering to the ground. He stood still, like a statue in his pose, concerned that his error would alert the residents of the house to his presence. At first there was silence then laughter again came from the house above. He was safe and carefully he moved back to the window.

"I'm going to wait till it calms down upstairs. By the sounds of things the fuckers are enjoying our loot. It shouldn't be too long before they turn in for the night. You two go back to the van and wait for me. Take Joni with you and be ready to leave in a hurry when I get back," he whispered.

"How will we know when you're coming back?" Ed asked.

"Oh you'll know alright!" came Ged's reply, his words accompanied with a sinister smile.

For several hours Ged sat quietly in the cellar with nothing but an old dust sheet wrapped around him for warmth. Alone with his thoughts he ran through his plan. He was to wait for the house to fall silent as this most likely meant that the people upstairs had taken to their beds. Then he would find the light switch and, using the petrol he had sniffed out earlier, he would burn the house down, along with every fucker inside. He had thought out every possible scenario of how this would be played out and they all had the same outcome. Everyone would die and he would have his revenge.

Then he heard a key turn in the lock of the cellar door and a bright light flooded his vision. Having spent several hours sat in relative darkness he now found himself blind such was the intense brightness. Luckily, he had hidden behind one of the generators and was not noticed by Jonathon as he drunkenly stumbled down the steep stairway.

"Cheese beer, cheese beer, lovely, lovely cheese beer!" Jonathon sang to himself.

His vision returned, Ged sat still, quietly listening to Jonathon's drunken song. Although unable to see him, he reasoned that by the tone of his voice he was young, and what's more he was intoxicated. But was he alone? He had not factored anyone entering the cellar into his plans and was not prepared to make a move unless he was 100% sure.

"Bunch of lightweights, taking the knock like that and falling asleep. The night is yet young and there is cheese beer to be drunk. Where are you cheese beer? There you are and you are all mine!" Jonathon slurred, spying the large keg of Butty's homebrew and drunkenly staggering towards it.

This was it, the boy was alone. Ged shifted himself slightly, ready to make his move. He looked to the floor and saw a shadow approaching then he heard the sound of beer gushing from the keg tap filling an empty pint glass. Now was the time.

He stepped out from behind the generator and found himself behind Jonathon who was bent forward and swaying slightly, filling his glass with beer from the keg. He swiftly swung his arm around the boy's neck, placing him into a choke hold. Jonathon was too drunk to defend himself and in no time at all he was unconscious. Ged looked over his victim.

"I've got plans for you young man," he said.

He dragged Jonathon to the window and pushed him through the small opening. Spying the many petrol canisters he had smelt out earlier, manically he emptied them one by one, covering as much of the cellar as he could.

Pouring the remains of the final canister, he moved towards the window and flicked open the lid on his zippo lighter, stroking his thumb against the flint wheel. Eyes wide, he glared into the flickering flame, adrenaline pumping through his body.

"Time to burn!" he growled.

Journal Entry 13

"Ace get up, we've got to move NOW!" Dave yelled, shaking me into consciousness.

My head was spinning in a drunken slumber from the vodka and Butty's cheesy home brew. I opened my eyes to see a shadowy figure before me. It was Dave but his features were masked by a haze of smoke. At first I thought it was the alcohol making my vision groggy. Then the intense heat and smell of burning hit me.

"What the hell is going on? Where's Emily?" I panicked, quickly scouting the room, looking for my daughter.

"She's fine John, she's with Butty. We've got to go now. Come on lar, shift your fucking arse, the whole house is in flames and I'll be damned if we're burning with it!" Dave replied.

Dave helped me to my feet and, stumbling over empty beer bottles, we made our way out onto the hallway. Flames rose from the ground floor, spreading up the walls towards the ceiling. In my hazy state it looked almost beautiful. The vibrant orange glow of fire danced across the hallway, igniting the woodchip walls and releasing thunderous crackling sounds. It was an ear popping song that stood in contrast to the elegant sway of the flames. I tried to comprehend how this could have happened. Did Dave or Butty fall asleep whilst smoking and drop a lit cigarette? Did someone attempt to drunkenly cook up some spam after getting a case of late night munchies? Neither seemed likely, as the fire looked to have started on the ground floor before quickly spreading to engulf the rest of the house.

We rushed into the spam store room; smouldering cans of hot salty meat unleashed smells that reminded me of summer BBQ's. It smelt sublime in there but the intense heat was quickly making breathing difficult. On the floor, next to a particularly hot pile of tins, lay my journal with smoke smouldering from one of its corners. I took it in my hands quickly and patted out any potential for fire.

The window was already open and I could see the rope ladder had been lowered. I looked out of the window. It was dark and the glow of fire burning up the exterior of the house blinded my vision. I couldn't see anything past the window but one thing I was sure of was the rope ladder was no more having been swallowed by the fire. All that remained were the singed ends wrapped around the hooks drilled into the window sill.

"Jump!"

I heard a voice shout in the distance. It sounded like Butty but the noise from the blaze meant I could not be sure.

"Jump you daft prick!"

It was definitely Butty.

"Come on Ace we'll do it together!" Dave said, confidently moving forward to join me at the window.

We both climbed up onto the window ledge, the flames close enough to tickle our feet. Dave placed a cigarette into his mouth then bent down to light it from the fire below. The cool bastard. He was still wearing his sunglasses too! We gave each other a knowing nod. Words were not needed. We jumped and landed just short of the thick brambles and wooden stakes we had hammered into the ground that morning.

"Are you ok Ace? Can you walk?" Dave asked.

Surprisingly I was fine. By some miracle my back had held out and I was good to go. I nodded my response and hurriedly we made our way up the steep steps to Weston Road. There I saw Emily with her Uncle in front of the Ford Thunderbird, watching as his house burnt to the ground. I ran to her and took her in my arms. Twice in two days I feared I had lost her and I did not want to let her go.

"Emily thank God you're OK," I said tearfully.

Emily looked past me and beyond Dave to the steps we had just climbed, waiting for someone else to appear.

"Where is he, where's Jonathon? Dad where's Jonathon? Why isn't he with you? He should be with you!" Emily panicked, becoming more hysterical with every word.

"I checked every room Ace, we were the only 2 left in there I'm sure of it," Dave said.

"Well then where is he?" Emily screamed.

Above the roar of the fire we heard the revving of a vehicle engine and bright headlights beamed along the road, illuminating our position. In the road ahead was a large blue transit van and on top stood a lone figure, holding in his hand what looked to be a decapitated head.

"Who the hell is that and what is he holding? Is that a head?" I said, holding a hand to my forehead in an attempt to shield my eyes from the blinding headlights.

"Fuck me!" Dave exclaimed before giving a knowing glance to Butty.

"Well I don't know the lunatic holding it but me and Dave have seen that head before. Only it was attached to shoulders last time we saw it," Butty informed.

"It's the dick head we told you about, the one that knocked himself out falling from the van we looted. That looks like the same van too," Dave added.

"Hello fuckers!" shouted the man on top of the van. "How are we this evening? Enjoying the bonfire I hope? This here is my cousin Joni. I believe some of you have already had the pleasure of his company?" he added, referring to the decaying head in his hand.

I could see the rage building inside of my brother. His home and our safety had been destroyed. Everything he had worked towards to protect us from the apocalypse was burning down before us. But why? What had we possibly done to this man to warrant his actions?

Then the man turned from us and began a conversation with the head he was holding. The crackle of the fire was too loud for me to make out what he was saying but it appeared as if the head had reminded him of something he needed to say and he turned again to face us.

"Oh and I almost forgot, you can thank Joni here for reminding me. I do believe someone appears to be missing from your little group. Any ideas people? Come along speak up, I haven't got all evening," the man shouted.

"Jonathon!" Emily screamed, making a move to run towards the van.

I wrapped my arms around her waist, preventing my daughter from running. Emily kicked and wriggled in an attempt to break free, screaming her boyfriend's name but there was not a chance I was letting her go.

"An eye for an eye. You take from me, I take from you. See you around fuckers!" The man shouted before climbing down from on top of the van then entering through the passenger door.

The blue transit performed a U-turn then opened its rear doors sending two figures tumbling out on to the road. The van then sped away, down towards Weston Point. It took a few moments for my eyes to adjust to the darkness but when they did I saw that the two figures were zombies and they were shuffling towards a street light. A street light that had a man tied to it. It was Jonathon.

The four of us ran to Jonathon as fast as we could but we were too far away to reach him before the zombies did. We could only watch with despair as they tore through his shirt then, digging their hands into his stomach, ripped through his skin and pulled out his intestines and shovelled them into their pale rotting mouths. The poor lad's screams filled the air.

Butty was the first to Jonathon. A well placed boot to the head sent one of the zombies tumbling away and using his bare hands, he grabbed the other by its hair and dragged it from our friend. He then repeatedly brought a knee crashing into the zombie's face; teeth, flesh, bone and gore flew in every direction.

A hysterical Emily was the next to arrive, grabbing her boyfriend's spilled intestines from the ground and pushing them back into his stomach through his open wound. Repeatedly she cried "Please don't die" and her shaking hands struggled to secure the slippery entrails in place.

Dave ran past Emily to the zombie Butty had thwarted and stomped on its head until it was no more.

I was the last to make it to Jonathon and he was no longer screaming when I got there. Almost lifeless, his head hung down with blood seeping from his mouth. Emily continued to press her hands hard against the large tear in his stomach, attempting to stop the content from falling out. With eyes closed tight she begged for her boyfriend to live. He summoned enough strength to lift his head and with eyes struggling to stay open he looked to me. He looked apologetic, like he felt he had failed us. Almost devoid of life he wheezed his last word.

"Sorry."

Then Jonathon was dead. Emily screamed in despair. All of her pain and anger manifested into a high pitched cry that sent my vision blurry and caused my head to rattle. If any survivors in the vicinity had heard then surely they would have believed that there was a new breed of zombie roaming the streets. One that made the current rotting bastards seem like kittens in comparison.

Butty removed a knife from his boot and stepped up to Jonathon. We all knew what needed to be done and my brother being well, my brother, decided to take the responsibility. Only, before he could complete the act, Emily took the knife from her uncle's hand. Not one of us argued with her. Her face held a look that said she would not be deterred and this was something she felt she needed to do.

Emily took her boyfriend's lifeless head in her hands and lifted it so that his chin was no longer resting on his chest. She looked into his eyes and told him she loved him then whispered something into his ear before saying "I promise". She then stabbed the knife through his forehead, penetrating the brain, removing any chance of him reanimating as a zombie. Like a little girl lost she flung her arms around me and sobbed into my chest. There was nothing I could say to make things better. All I could do was hold her.

"We've got to get moving Ace. I much as I hate to say it, we've got to go," Dave said.

"He's right little brother. The fire and noise will have alerted both people and zombies alike to our presence. We've got to get off the streets and find somewhere safe to regroup and figure out what we're going to do," Butty added.

I carried Emily in my arms and followed Butty and Dave as they rushed to the Thunderbird.

"Wanking fucking cunts!" Dave shouted, booting the side of the car.

All four tyres had been slashed, leaving us with no alternative but to walk. Butty opened the boot of the car and retrieved 2 large holdall bags. He opened one of them to reveal several crowbars, knives, limited food supplies (spam), bin bags, a med kit and a few bottles of water as well as a walkie-talkie. My brother passed out the weapons and Dave glared at his crowbar with disdain then looked over to the burning house wistfully.

"It might be ok? I think I should go in and take a look, just to make sure," he said.

"Dave it's made of plastic. It's about as ok as the rest of my house. I told you that Battle Paddle of yours was a terrible weapon. It will be nothing more than a boiling puddle of plastic by now. You're better off with a crowbar anyway. It has got multiple uses such as prying open locked doors, smashing windows, removing nails and of course its main function, twatting zombies. Plus it's easy to carry unlike that giant spoon of yours," Butty replied.

Dejected and mourning the loss of Jonathon, his Battle Paddle and the use of the Thunderbird, Dave lit a cigarette and placed his earphones over his head then reached down to his Sony Walkman cassette player, searching for the play button. Only the play button could not be found. His hand fumbled in panic as he unclipped the Walkman from his belt and brought it up to his face to inspect what was now a misshaped rectangle of melted plastic. I have never seen Dave look so upset. I mean he almost dropped the cigarette from his mouth and that is something he has never done. He was so distraught he couldn't speak and I swear I saw a tear fall from behind his sunglasses.

"Put these on, just rip a hole for your head," Butty instructed, passing everyone a bin bag.

"What are these for?" I asked.

Butty opened the second holdall to reveal the horrific content. If was full of zombie limbs, many of which had been linked together with rope.

"The bin bags are to keep your clothes from getting covered in zombie splodge. The limbs are to keep us alive. There should be enough for all of us, the holdall is pretty big and I filled it the best I could. Grab a limb link and drape it over your shoulders. The smell should be enough to mask our scent," Butty explained.

Great, limb links. The nutter had given a name to his creation.

Butty took my diary and placed it in the holdall. He then ripped a hole in one of the bin bags and placed it over Emily's head. She was still in my arms and in no fit state to do anything for herself. My brother then placed a limb link around her neck, caring not that the disgusting and stinking zombie parts were touching my clothes. There was even a rotting hand in my face and I was dangerously close to having my nose picked by a decaying finger. Noticing the squirming as I tried to move my nose away from the demon digit, Butty frowned, shook his head and snapped the finger clean from the zombie hand. I was half expecting him to ram the thing up my nose and if we had not had suffered such a loss, I suspect that would have been the outcome.

"As long as you're carrying Emily little brother I don't think you'll be needing a limb link so I'll keep yours in the hold all for now. Right then, follow me. We need to get off the streets. Once we've done that, we'll figure out what we're going to do next," Butty said.

We quickly moved along Weston Road in the opposite direction to that of the psycho in the blue van. Butty had gone into survival mode and was leading from the front, rushing ahead to check for zombies then giving us a thumbs up when the coast was clear. It would appear to anyone looking in that Butty was taking the loss of his home and Jonathon with some ease but I knew different. Avoidance was his coping mechanism. He would rather concentrate on the here and now and what needed to be done rather than think about all he had lost. Knowing my brother as well as I did, supressing his feelings would only last for so long and pretty soon, his pain and anger would rise to the surface and not without consequence.

I had never seen Dave look so depressed. His quick succession of losses was like taking body shots from a champion boxer. The first blow being the house, the second Jonathon, the third the Thunderbird, the fourth his Battle Paddle and the fifth and knockout blow was his melted Sony Walkman. I didn't know this Dave. His confidence, swagger and cool-as-can-be persona had gone. What remained was a man lost, a shell of his former self. I just hoped he could find a way back to us. Dave's energy and "Fuck the apocalypse" attitude was going to be needed now more than ever.

Emily quietly sobbed into my chest as I carried her along Weston Road, past the Cenotaph War Memorial and on to Greenway Road. She had not uttered a word since stabbing the knife through Jonathon's head. She too was lost, swallowed by grief and anger. It's difficult to explain the hurt I felt seeing her like this and knowing there was nothing I could do or say to make things better was heart wrenching. She had suffered a great loss, we all had, and our little group was in desperate need of some luck.

Butty rushed ahead, signalling for us to stay put whilst he turned left onto Balfour Street. I could hear the sounds of his knife penetrating undead skulls and the slurping noises that accompanied its retraction. After several minutes he returned, out of breath but with a glimmer of hope in his eyes.

"Hurry, I think I've found a place for us to go. Barry's is open!" he said.

God could have appeared right there and then and told me this whole apocalypse was just a joke, clicked his fingers then made everything go away and I would not have been as surprised as I was to hear my brother say that Barry's was open.

BJ & J Owen's, or Barry's as it is more commonly known, is a small newsagents on Balfour Street. Growing up just a short walk away, Butty and I would frequent Barry's to spend our pocket money on treats such as sweets, chocolates and pop. In fact, every Saturday Butty would try to buy a porno magazine or 'Grumble' Mag as he calls them. Splosh was his particular favourite. He did this from about the age of twelve and Barry would always take it as far as he could, leading Butty to believe he was going to get his sweaty little palms on the latest publication of Splosh. Only, when it came to paying he would just laugh and chuck him a 10p mix of sweets for being a cheeky shit. Years that went on for and as far as I know, Butty never got his hands on a copy. For those of you not familiar with this top shelf publication, Splosh specialises in naked women covered in cake. Very tongue in cheek which, coincidently, is the name of my brothers other favourite 'Grumble' magazine. When Butty reached eighteen years of age Barry still wouldn't sell it to him as turning him down on a weekly basis had become tradition and it always made him laugh. Even if over the years it had cost him a small fortune in sugary cola bottles, jelly sweets and flying saucers.

Barry and his little store of magical items has been part of my life for as long as I can remember. You could go in there with a shopping list of fuse wire, sewing cotton, toilet roll, milk, a book of raffle tickets, Pot Noodle, dust clothes and an ice lolly and you would get everything plus about four others items you never knew you wanted. It was his stock and friendly service that made Barry's better than the rest and secured the shop's longevity in this town. The last thing I was expecting to hear was that, in the middle of a zombie apocalypse, he was still open.

We followed Butty onto Balfour Street; street lights illuminated the many zombie corpses littering the road. It looked like a war zone. Abandoned cars and boarded up houses filled our vision.

"I can't take full credit for this but the four over there were mine. The rest were dead already. Walk carefully. There may be a zombie lying amongst the dead just waiting to reach out and grab you. Unless they are a threat, leave them be. There's no point using up energy for no reason so save your strength and no wandering off just to kill a zombie. We're not keeping a kill score here so don't go putting yourself in danger for no reason. Besides, if we were keeping score I would be out in front by a country mile. If you do find yourself having to engage one and they are on the ground, use the heel of your boot and stomp down hard on their heads. It's the quickest way to kill them. I wouldn't use a weapon unless you have to. I'll take the lead so if you follow in my steps we should be alright. You may be tempted to bang on the doors of the many boarded up houses. Don't. These are dangerous times and people will protect their homes and families with their lives if need be. They may not take kindly to strangers looking for shelter in their homes. Barry's has its lights on and the sign on the door says open. The reason I think Barry is alive and this is our best option is the graffiti on the window says 'NO ZOMBIES'. That's good enough for me. Everyone ready?" he said.

Butty's resilience was inspiring. There he was having just lost his home and he was able to put it out of his mind and focus on what needed to be done. If I'm honest I was struggling, only managing to keep my head above water for Emily. She was in real pain and I needed to be strong for the both of us. Luckily, I had my brother. His actions and leadership helped me to pick myself up, to suck it up and carry on the best I could, for Emily more than anything. Dave was another story. Everything that made Dave 'Dave' was gone, lost to the fire. Seeing my friend so lost and withdrawn was upsetting. I had never seen him like this before. Shit I doubt Dave had ever known himself like this before. The only thing he had left was his cigarettes. In fact, I think it was only the fags stopping him from doing a full on Michael Douglas from Falling Down.

With Emily in my arms and Dave behind me, we carefully followed Butty along Balfour Street, avoiding the carpet of dead bodies that lay across the road. As we edged closer to Barry's the more bodies we encountered and man they were a diverse bunch of corpses. There was a transvestite with one arm, what appeared to be one of Barry's paperboys and a rather large naked old lady with a push bike on top of her. It was quite the collection.

Now directly in front of the newsagents, I looked upon the spray painted window and the door to the shop with the 'Open' sign showing.

"I'll go in first; Barry and I go way back. Hopefully he won't get spooked if he sees it's me," Butty reasoned.

With his hand behind his back and knife gripped tightly, Butty cautiously opened the shop door and stepped inside. I heard him mumble something and then clear as day I heard Barry laugh and shout the following...

"Bloody hell Butty, it's the end of the world and you're still trying to buy a copy of Splosh you dirty sod!"

Butty popped his head out of the door and, looking rather sheepish, he motioned for us to come in. Inside it was business as usual. The shelving units were fully stocked with Barry's marvellous collection of snacks, magazines, canned drinks that you thought were discontinued years ago and of course all the little things you cannot buy from any place else that make a shop like this a life safer.

"Now then, what can I get you?" Barry said with a smile from behind his counter.

"You know you really should lock that door?" I said.

"Nonsense! Just because we're living in a zombie apocalypse it doesn't mean people no longer need their local newsagents. What are they going to do when they run out of toilet paper? Only 25p for an individual roll here. Or what about when the cold weather disappears and all the decaying zombies start stinking up the place? 89p for a can of air freshener and it's 2 for 1 at the moment! You can't beat those prices. Now then, you guys look like you've been through a lot. I'd say food and a refreshing drink will sort you out. So that's four Pot Noodles and four cans of Lucozade... that will be £6.48 please and I'll boil a kettle for your pot noodles for free. How's about that?" Barry said.

"Actually he's right John, when you think about it there is no need to lock the door. The large amount of dead outside is enough to mask any living scent and zombies are not exactly known for their co-ordination. I'll eat my smalls if I ever see one of them manage a door handle and we all know how dirty my duds are. Even if one does manage to come in I'm sure Barry could take care of it and judging by the dead bastards outside you already have done. You've got a good set up here Barry and you're right. Apocalypse or not, people still need to wipe their arseholes and fill their bellies. Plus it's small enough for looters to pass by. Most will be hitting the larger stores and won't think to loot the smaller places like this. Everyone knows you around here as well and loyalty and trust means a lot, even if it is the end of the world. You keep that door unlocked and serve this community till your stock runs out. But food and drink are not what we need. We need somewhere to stay for the night. We were attacked. We've lost our home and a life too. They burnt down my house and one of our own was taken and murdered right in front of us. All we ask is that we stay here for one night and we'll be on our way first thing in the morning. As soon as the sun comes up we'll be gone but it's too dangerous for us to travel at night, especially on foot. What do you say?" Butty asked.

Barry lifted the hatch in his counter and walked to the shop door, locking it then changing the sign in the window to 'Closed'. He then moved over to the magazine section of the shop and retrieved a copy of Splosh from the top shelf then handed it to Butty.

"Stay as long as you need," he said.

We sat in the store room of BJ & J Owens whilst its owner described everything that had happened to him since the outbreak. We got to know about his encounter with the paperboy, his regulars turning into zombies and trying to eat him, the cyclist that came in yesterday asking for help and his superhero girlfriend that came looking for him. Barry even let us have the Pot Noodles and drinks for free. Now I'm not exactly a fan of the freeze dried nutrition free grot pots but it was a damn sight more appealing than facing another tin of my brother's spam, of which he still carried a small supply. Dave was a man without identity, offering one word answers and shoulder shrugs as responses to questions. Emily had still not spoken a word since Jonathon's death but she was no longer sobbing and instead sat quietly on the floor, hugging her legs whilst hiding her face behind her hair. It was a quiet and subdued evening but I sensed Barry was glad of the company and we were most definitely appreciative of his hospitality.

As the evening progressed I noticed Butty was in deep thought. He was a simple man and easy to work out. His silence combined with his eyes flicking from side to side meant he was working out our next move. I had to ask.

"What are you thinking brother?" I said.

"I'm thinking that tomorrow we rebuild. We've all been through a lot today but we do not have time to grieve and mourn what we have lost, not yet anyway. We need to move forward and quickly. Tomorrow we find a new place. Somewhere secure and we start again. I've got a place in mind but I need to give it some more thought so I suggest we rest the best we can and in the morning we'll discuss it further. Everyone agree?" he said.

Dave nodded a solemn reply whilst sucking down on a cigarette.

"I think you're right. We need to rest, take stock then tomorrow we move out. Emily, what do you think?" I asked.

Emily slowly lifted her head and spoke for the first time since Jonathon's death.

"What do I think? I think the man that did this to us, that burnt down our home and killed Jonathon, has made a massive mistake. He might not know it yet, in fact he's probably feeling pretty happy with himself right now, but soon he'll come to realise that he fucked with the wrong people. So here's what I think. I think he's a fucking dead man! A fucking dead man walking!"

Then the power went out.

F-T-B

In the heart of Runcorn Old Town was Rockwell's, a 1950s Rock n Roll themed diner. With music memorabilia covering the walls, Wurlitzer Jukeboxes and custom booths made from fairground waltzer seating, the diner stood out in a town desperate for something different, offering an alternative to the many take away joints and chip shops in the area. It was a place where people could go to escape and be transported to another time whilst enjoying good food and an atmosphere filled with American nostalgia with just a hint of British culture in the form of a red English phone booth. Inside the phone booth stood a life size, pouting statue of Marilyn Monroe.

The diner's tribute nights in particular were very popular with customers and the night the dead began to roam the earth, the packed out diner had planned to treat their patrons to an Elvis impersonator, complete with a full backing band. Only, the band had become ill moments before they were due to play and Elvis was nowhere to be seen. Luckily, Chris Unsworth, Ben Argyle, Tim Daniel and Ricky Moss, also known as punk rockers Faster than Bulls, were in attendance celebrating the recording of their new EP 'Can You Hear Me?' When they offered to step in and entertain the restless patrons, the last thing they expected was for their music to be the accompaniment to a zombie outbreak.

It was Chris Morris, a chef at the diner that brought the infection to Rockwell's. It was his first shift since returning from a horrendous lad's holiday to Riga, the party capital of Latvia. Twelve had set off for four days of debauchery and only Chris returned. The rest of his friends, having been taken ill, were hospitalised and he never saw them again. He had only been home a few hours when the diner requested he come in to work to cover for his colleague Bev Kruger who had called in sick that night. Reluctantly he had agreed, not wanting to let his friends and colleagues down. One of the last things he did before being killed by his co-worker and fellow chef Matty Guy was to prepare the complimentary popcorn. It was tradition at Rockwell's that every customer received a free bowl of popcorn before their meal. Little did the customers know that Chris, whilst suffering a heavy nose bleed, sneezed over the popcorn before it was served and small speckles of blood landed on the complimentary snack, leading to the infection spreading. The only people to turn down the free offering was Faster than Bulls as Ricky hated the stuff and wouldn't have it anywhere near him, stating "It makes my piss sting and smell like gravy. Even looking at the stuff makes my widge tingle!" It was a decision that saved their lives and from their position on stage they watched as, one by one, everyone became violently ill.

It was an easy decision for Faster than Bulls to agree to play Rockwell's at such short notice. They had only recently left the recording studio and had their instruments with them. Plus they were in their element performing and felt at home entertaining people, even if the audience had expected to see Elvis and not a Punk Rock band. Chris, the bands bassist and front man, loved a challenge and he was relishing in the task of winning everyone over. Only, they didn't have a chance to convert the rock n roll loving diners into Bulls & Bullettes as half way through their first track 'Blowout', there was an incident at Table 1 where a large gentleman with a pale complexion projectile vomited directly into the mouth of his girlfriend who in turn, vomited into the lap of her mother. The mother had worse problems than her daughter's puke to deal with though as an excruciating pain stabbed through her lower abdomen and bowels, causing a severe case of diarrhoea.

Green acidy puke and deep red excrement poured from Table 1 as nearby customers screamed and ran from the disgusting river of bodily fluids heading their way. There was no escape as one by one each table fell ill and in no time at all, Rockwell's was full of people puking and shitting for Queen and Country. The band, to their credit, kept playing, providing a rock out sound track to the disgusting barf and shit-a-thon. It was only when Chris noticed that one of the customers, a small slight man wearing a Teddy Boy red suit with black trim, had stopped being ill and was looking right at him. Something about this man was different. Even with his puke covered face he looked dissimilar to the others. He was gaunt, with pale grey skin revealing thin veins that stretched across his face. But what really caught Chris' attention were the man's white glazed eyes. They were truly unhuman and sent a chill straight to the frontman's core. Still, he continued to play and sing without taking his eyes from the man in the Teddy Boy suit who returned the stare and slowly moved towards the stage with thick saliva pouring from his open mouth. Chris' exterior remained calm; however, inside he was anything but and was mentally preparing to defend himself.

Kicking out, he pushed a foot into the man's chest, sending him tumbling backwards to the ground. He looked to his band mates for support but they hadn't noticed a thing and instead were watching the customers continue to fall ill and collapse at their tables. Then the man rose to his feet and again advanced forward, his white glazed eyes fixed on his target. The warning kick achieved nothing and Chris now looked for a permanent solution. He looked down to the Gibson SG bass guitar in his arms and quickly dismissed his thought. He loved his guitar too much to use it as a weapon. He looked across to the bass amplifier. If it had been his own Mark Bass amp, there would not have been a chance in hell he would have taken his next course of action.

With the stalker Teddy Boy almost within touching distance, Chris, summoning all his strength, picked up the bass amp and brought it down on top of the man's head. The metal mesh covering the speaker spliced his head like prime beef pushed through a mince meat grinder.

Chris, now unable to provide bass guitar to the band's music, continued to sing as he looked down at the man he had just killed, his bloodied pulp of a head now the same colour as his red suit.

Ricky, wearing his trade mark sheepskin Cossack hat, was aware something was going on with his band mate but he was focused on Table 7 and the woman ripping the throat out of her boyfriend's neck with her teeth. It didn't appear real and he was mesmerised as she gnashed through his skin, scoffing on the man's tendons and cartilage feverishly like she hadn't eaten for a week.

Ben was sat at his drum kit, pounding the skins forcefully. The harder he played, the further he hoped he would become lost in the music so that he could ignore what was happening. He had witnessed two small children, twin girls of no more than eight years of age with pale complexions, grey eyes and jet black hair, die then come back to life. He watched as they ripped their mother to pieces then proceeded to shovel her shredded body into their mouths. They had made short work of their mother and were hungry for more. They were hungry for Ben!

No matter how hard he concentrated on his drumming he could still see the girls slowly heading his way, their mother's blood coating their mouths and identical sunflower patterned dresses. He looked to Chris who, although still singing, was transfixed with the sliced face of the dead Teddy Boy. He called to Ricky but he was mesmerised with what was playing out at Table 7. Finally he turned to Tim and, like the rest of the band, he continued to play but had his eyes set on a mammoth of a man wearing a chef's uniform. He was enormous, with a head as wide as his shoulders and he was eating his way through the screaming customers as they headed for the exit.

The devil twins edged closer and Ben's drumming became erratic as he found it harder to ignore the imminent threat.

"Fuck this shit!" he yelled then ceased pounding his drums and unscrewed the top nut from his hi-hat cymbal.

Taking the cymbal in his hand, he launched it towards the girls like a Frisbee. Chris saw the cymbal as it skimmed past his head and both he and Ben watched as it hit one of the girls in her forehead and sliced through her skull.

The loss of her sister did nothing to deter the remaining devil twin and, with thick gloops of saliva falling from her gnashing mouth, she moved closer to her target. Ben moved from behind his drum kit, ran past the rest of his band mates and stabbed the girl through her eye with one of his drumsticks. Even with the music playing he could still hear her eyeball pop.

"Look out!" Chris yelled down the microphone as behind Ben approached the previously absent Elvis impersonator wearing a gold jump suit covered in excrement, chomping and ripping at the cheek of a decapitated head.

Ben turned quickly, slipping in a puddle of blood and bodily fluids then falling to the floor. Zombie Elvis closed in, dropping the half eaten head in favour of a fresher meal.

Rushing to help his friend, Chris pulled the drum stick out of the dead girl's eye and repeatedly stabbed Zombie Elvis in the side of his head, causing dark blood to spurt from the small circular wounds.

"Where the hell do you think he's been hiding?" Ben asked, lifting himself up from the puddle of human waste.

"Judging by the kip of him and the shit on his jump suit I'd say he did the real Elvis proud and died on the toilet. What the fuck is going on Benji? Everyone's dying then coming back!" Chris said.

"Do I really have to spell it out for you?" Ben replied.

Chris turned to Ricky and Tim who continued to play their guitars, Ricky still taken with the action at Table 7 and Tim watching the huge chef as he devoured the remaining customers that had tried to escape.

"This is your fault Ricky. Let's go to Runcorn you said, it'll be an experience you said," Chris complained.

"I'd call this an experience wouldn't you?" Ricky replied.

"Heads up, massive bastard chef alert," Tim warned, alerting the others to the threat heading their way.

Matty Guy, the behemoth head chef from Rockwell's, had quickly devoured the unfortunate customers that had tried to escape and was now set on the only survivors left in the diner. His once white uniform had become a deep red and it clung to his body, making his hulking frame all the more intimidating.

"If you two would like to stop playing your guitars it would be much appreciated. I reckon it'll take all of us to put this fella down," Ben offered, brandishing his remaining drumstick as a weapon.

Both Ricky and Tim stopped playing and joined their band mates to face the huge zombie chef heading their way. Ricky was the first to react, running at the big man and smashing him in the face with his Fender Stratocaster. The blow would have been enough to inflict considerable damage to anyone but not Matty. It hardly made a dent. Ricky's guitar however was ruined and was almost in two pieces. He looked down at his beloved instrument in shock, partly because it was broken but mostly because his plan hadn't worked.

Next up it was Tim and, wielding his Telecaster guitar, he had the same idea as Ricky but, rather than smash it into the big guys face, he brought it crashing down on top of his head. The impact caused Tim's body to vibrate and his vision blur. When his vision returned, he looked upon his broken Telecaster and the intact head of the encroaching chef.

"What's this guy made of, fucking steel?" Tim questioned.

Behind the intimidating bulk of the zombie chef, Chris noticed the doors to the diner's kitchen were open and an idea formulated.

"Lads, give me a hand, quickly! I know what to do with Massive Bastard here," Chris requested.

They upturned one of the diner's tables and using it as a battering ram, ran at the chef, sending him backwards into the kitchen, shutting the doors then moving the large traditional red British telephone box in front of them for added safety.

They stood with their backs against the phone booth which shook violently due to the constant banging and pushing against the kitchen doors by the gigantic, newly named Massive Bastard. In front of them lay the dead, the dying and the undead with the latter slowly heading their way. Ricky collected a selection of knives and forks from the table closest and handed them to his band mates.

"Stab them in the head lads and don't let them scratch or bite you. This is going to sound fucking absurd but I think we're dealing with zombies boys. I don't know what else to call this but I'll tell you what, we ain't dying tonight, no fucking way!" Ricky yelled.

"I'll take the guy at Table 4 that looks like JFK," said Chris, marching to his target.

"The old dear sucking on her husband, she's mine. It looks like she's lost her false teeth and I doubt I can get infected from a gumming," Ben informed, readying his knife for action.

"I'll take the zombie waitress," Ricky said walking towards his undead victim.

Tim looked at the knife in his hand and then to the pregnant women at table 6, snarling and gnashing her teeth as she lifted her head out of the torso of a male customer.

"Forgive me," he begged, before running at the pregnant women and stabbing her repeatedly in the head.

For Faster than Bulls, it was the start of a very long night.

Chris scribbled tirelessly. Since the carnage of the previous night he'd done nothing but write down lyric after lyric, pausing only to demand his bandmates bring more napkins for him to pen what would be without doubt the bands greatest record. The massacre at Rockwell's Diner had ignited a creative spark the likes he had never experienced and he vividly remembered every moment of the night's horrendous events. But rather than feel fear or shock at the death and destruction that surrounded him, he was overcome with excitement. He was excited because every death told a story - stories that were shaping the lyrics to the band's next album.

"More napkins!" Chris barked.

Ricky sat slumped in a white and red leather striped seat that was once a fairground bumper car. His head, snug inside his sheepskin Cossack hat, rested in a puddle of congealed blood on the table in front of him. After hours of trying, he had finally fallen asleep only to be woken minutes later by his bandmate's demands for more napkins.

"Get them yourself!" Ricky said, his head remaining on the table. "Fuck me, Chris, you've got legs, get off your arse and use them. Do you know how long you've been sat there, writing away, ignoring us all? Eighteen Fucking hours. Eighteen hours and the only time you open your mouth is to demand more napkins. Well you can fuck off!"

"I am writing our next album! This needs my full and uninterrupted attention. The words are flowing like a lyrical tsunami and you want me to stop? I've never felt so alive man, what I've got here is going to take us to the next level. It's cosmic dude! Now stop sulking and bring me some more napkins," Chris asked.

"No. Fuck off!" came the stern reply.

"Ricky!" Chris yelled, banging his fist hard against the table.

"Sit on it!" Ricky instructed, lifting both hands and presenting Chris with his middle fingers.

Chris looked across to Ben, who was sat quietly behind what remained of his drum kit, watching the argument escalate. Ben could tell by the mischievous look on his friend's face what he was going to do.

"Don't Chris," Ben pleaded.

"Hey Ricky…" Chris said.

"Chris don't," Ben again implored.

"Hey Ricky, you know that stupid hat you love so much? Well you might want to take better care where you rest your head dude and maybe pick a table with less zombie splodge on it," Chris sniggered.

Ricky lifted his head from the table and thick gloops of blood dripped from his hat. He quickly removed it from his head and inspected the damage. It was ruined and a smiling Chris caught his eye. Enraged he ran at his band mate, paying little attention to the thick slippery soup of zombie waste on the floor. He fell face down, the momentum sending him skidding past Chris and crashing into the red English phone booth pushed up against the doors of the diner's kitchen, almost knocking the life size Marilyn Monroe statue inside out of the booth's door. The doors to the kitchen began to shake and the moans of the undead could be heard from inside.

"Great, you've woke up Massive Bastard. We've been keeping quiet for a reason you know? The last thing we want is to deal with him again." Ben complained.

"He's right Ricky, keep the noise down will you and hurry up with those napkins, you're stunting my creativity," Chris said.

Ricky picked himself up; his clothes, covered in gore, now clung to his skin. He removed his ruined hat and threw it in Chris' direction before sulking off to the diner's toilet area.

"Here you go mardy arse, write away," Ben said, walking over to Chris and passing him a new box of napkins.

Chris tore into the box and returned to writing. Ben, watching his friend feverishly work, reached for a napkin to read it, only for Chris to snatch it from his hands.

"No! You can't read it, not yet. Believe me when I say this stuff is going to blow your mind but you have to wait. It's a work in progress!" Chris said.

"I've never seen you like this before Chris. You started writing the minute we killed the last zombie and you haven't stopped since. Ricky is losing his mind, I'm well... I don't know what I am to be truthful, and Tim, well, he hasn't spoken for hours. He's sat himself behind the bar and he won't come out," Ben said.

No reply came from Chris, he didn't even acknowledge his friend's words.

"Chris? Are you listening to me? Your friends are losing the plot. It's all very well you writing the lyrics to the world's greatest songs but at this rate you'll have no band left to play the music. Also, in case you haven't noticed, there appears to be a zombie apocalypse going on. I don't think we'll be gigging any time soon!" Ben yelled in his friend's face.

The doors to the kitchen again began to shake and the moans from "Massive Bastard" filled Rockwell's. Ben and Chris both looked towards the doors with concern. After several nervous moments, the groans and shaking ceased.

"What I'm saying is you need to stop," Ben said quietly, "We need to be working together, figuring out what we're going to do next, not bickering and shouting."

Chris stopped writing and looked to his friend, his eyes tired and red.

"If I stop then this is real. I'm not ready for that, not yet," he said, tears welling in his eyes.

"Chris, nobody is ready. Nobody. But look what we did together. We should have died last night but we pulled together and killed every flesh hungry dead bastard in this place. Apart from the big guy locked in the kitchen that is. Now we have to pull together again and figure out what to do next. Please mate, just put the pen down," Ben said softly.

Ben could see the struggle in Chris' face, his hand shaking as finger by finger he released his grip on the pen.

"Now what?" Chris asked.

Before Ben could answer, Ricky returned wearing a black and white polkadot chic 1950s dress. Both Chris and Ben fell about laughing.

"Yeah ha-ha very funny I know. It's the only clothing I could find that was relatively clean!" he said taking a seat next to Chris. "Finally stopped writing I see. Why is it you only listen to Ben and never me?"

"Because Ben isn't dressed like Betty Boop!" Chris replied.

"OK chaps, we need to talk about what's happening. It's been long enough now since we were attacked; we can't carry on sitting around doing nothing. Look at this place. We are surrounded by dead people. Last night was horrific I know. Nobody should have had to do what we did. But soon the smell from these people will be unbearable so we have a decision to make. We either clear Rockwell's of these bodies then stay here or we leave and find out just how bad it is out there," Ben suggested.

"Say we do leave, what then? Where do we go? Home?" Ricky asked.

"Depends what it's like out there I suppose. No doubt the military have been called in. The first places they'll clear are the cities. Liverpool is closest, we could go there?" Chris said.

"It's a risk. What if this thing happened so quick the military didn't stand a chance? Then the most populated areas have the most infected. Walking into Liverpool could be suicide. Tim what do you think? Tim?" Ben said.

Tim had spent the last few hours sat behind the bar area of Rockwell's, leaning against the gas cylinders stored under the counter. He'd always been the quiet type and the end of the world had sent him deeper into himself, preferring his own company to that of his band mates. What he had seen and done the night before played heavy on his mind and he struggled to come to terms with his actions. He had collected the wallets and purses of the people he and his friends had killed and studied them keenly, so that he would always remember their names.

Jackie Parkes, Mark Rigby, Karen Horabin, Gill Wright, Alex Parkes, Lyndon Brocklesby, Shannon Greenhaigh to name a few.

These people only a day earlier had headed out for an evening of food and music and never returned home. Instead, their battered bodies and mashed heads littered the diner. Behind the bar was the only place Tim couldn't see blood and, as far he was concerned, his band mates could call his name all they wanted, he wasn't about to join them.

Why did he survive and they hadn't? What was so special about him and the rest of the band that they escaped infection? Why were they so lucky? Or maybe the dead were the lucky ones and those that survived were cursed. Destined to spend the rest of their days living a hell on Earth. To kill or be killed. Tim was starting to think the latter was true and that he and his friends would be better off dead.

"Tim!" Ben again shouted.

"Ah he isn't coming, just leave him be, he'll come out when he's ready," Ricky said, filling the front of his polkadot dress with napkins, giving him an ample bosom. "Hey Chris what do you reckon? Quite convincing cleavage I'd say? I see how you've been looking at me in this dress. I think a few more days stuck in this place and you'll have me bent over a table..."

"Can I kill him? I really want to kill him!" Chris asked of Ben, trying his best to ignore Ricky who was flaunting his new cleavage in front of him.

Ricky, continuing with his teasing, grabbed a tomato sauce bottle from the table and stroked it suggestively. Gently at first but quickly increasing his up and down hand movements until reaching a climax, squeezing the bottle tightly and projecting tomato sauce into the air whilst screaming his friend's name.

The noise caused more rumblings from inside the kitchen and the door shook, almost tipping over the red telephone booth placed to keep them secure. The door of the telephone booth flung open and the Marilyn Monroe statue inside fell forward, her head hitting the ground hard and landing between the legs of the dead John F Kennedy lookalike zombie.

"Happy birthday Mr President!" Ricky said, attempting a sultry tone.

Then Massive Bastard roared from inside the kitchen and burst through the doors as they flung open, knocking the phone booth to the floor.

"Nice one lads, now Massive Bastard is loose! You do remember how difficult it was to contain him last time?" Ben growled at Chris and Ricky.

Massive Bastard stumbled out of the kitchen and immediately began pursuing Chris, Ben and Ricky. The guys were panicked, with the Rockwell's chef appearing even bigger to them than he had the night before.

"Chris, whack him with your guitar!" Ricky instructed.

"No way, I'd rather shit glass that use my guitar!" he replied.

"If we make it out of this alive I'm sure that can be arranged!" Ricky replied.

Whilst Chris, Ricky and Ben bickered over what they were going to do, Tim appeared from behind the bar holding a box of matches and a bottle of Sambuca. He approached the chef from behind then emptied the bottled liquor over the big guys head, soaking his upper body. His action was enough for Massive Bastard to turn away from the others and face him.

"You will be the last. No more… NO MORE!" Tim screamed, lighting a match and tossing it toward the giant zombie.

They all watched and shaded their eyes as the chef ignited and the smell of burning flesh filled the diner. On fire the huge zombie shuffled towards Tim clumsily, banging into walls and tables as he moved, burning everything he touched.

"Go, get out of here!" Tim yelled to his bandmates, himself remaining still, his eyes firmly set on the approaching zombie.

The others exited the diner through a fire door close to the bar area leading out onto Public Hall Street, which lies adjacent to Church Street in Runcorn Old Town.

"Tim! What are you doing?" Ben shouted.

Tim turned to face his friends, behind him a smouldering diner and the approaching frame of Massive Bastard, his skin darkened and crisped from the flames that engulfed him. Tim looked to his friends and smiled solemnly then there was a huge explosion, powerful enough to lift Chris,

Ricky and Ben from their feet and propel them backwards. The fire inside Rockwell's had spread rapidly, igniting the gas cylinders stored behind the bar.

Chris lifted his head from the floor and looked at the smoke engulfed doorway.

"Tim!" he yelled.

Out of the doorway walked Massive Bastard still on fire but also minus an arm and with his chest cavity exposed. In his remaining hand he gripped a dismembered leg. It belonged to Tim and he chewed on it like a giant ham.

"No!" Chris screamed.

Ricky and Ben grabbed their friend, preventing him from running towards the flaming zombie and they moved him from the diner, rushing towards Church Street.

When they arrived there, Church Street was alive with the undead. Zombies that had been shuffling aimlessly now had the scent of the living and they were heading towards Faster than Bulls. If they wanted to survive then they needed to move and move quickly.

Behind them was a large sign that said 'Welcome to Runcorn'. Only someone had altered the words using blood. It now read 'Welcome to DEADcorn'.

"I hate this fucking town," Chris groaned.

Journal Entry 14

"Wakey wakey little brother," Butty whispered.

I was having a severe case of deja vu. It was almost twenty four hours since my brother woke me with the exact same words only this time instead of his crazy grin greeting me when I opened my eyes, his face was stern and serious. How long I had been asleep I did not know but after the lights went out following Emily's vengeful words, the store room of BJ & J Owens fell silent. After everything we had been through there was nothing left to say or do but rest. I can't speak for the others but for me, sleep did not come easy. Emily's words lit a fire within me the likes I had never felt before. She wanted revenge for what the man with the blue van had done to Jonathon and she wasn't alone. Butty, for all of his words of finding somewhere secure where we could start again had other ideas. He too wanted payback. When you've known my brother as long as I have, you can see through his lies. Everything he said about finding a new place to call home was him testing the water, to see if we wanted the same thing he did. Emily's response gave him all the confirmation he needed and I know why he had woken me. He thought I needed convincing but he was wrong.

We left the dark store room and entered the shop area of Barry's where 80s Dave was waiting, sat on the floor against the magazine shelving unit smoking a cigarette.

"I'm in," I said purposely.

"How do you know what I was going to say?" Butty replied with bafflement.

"Brother, you are as transparent as you are crazy. All that talk last night about finding a new place and starting again? Pull the other one! After what that guy did to Jonathon and to your home? No, this isn't over. Not by a long way," I replied.

"Don't forget my fucking Walkman and Battle Paddle lar. When I find the prick I'm going to grab that manky head he carries around and shove it so far up his arse the cunt will be walking like a... well, like a fucking cunt that's what! Sorry about the insult that was terrible. I can't think straight without my music," Dave moaned, frustrated with his appalling attempt at a threat.

"As I said, I'm in but on one condition. Emily has no part of this. You heard her last night, she's out for blood but I can't risk losing her. She's all I've got, apart from you two loony tunes of course," I said.

"Way ahead of you little bro. I had a word with Barry and he slipped some Night Nurse into her drink so she'll be out for hours. It's only a short walk back up to the house. With any luck the fire will be out by now and we can see if anything is worth salvaging. Then we come back and we plan what our next move will be. Hopefully, Emily will have calmed down a little and we can bring her round to our way of thinking that yes, this prick has to pay but we need to plan and be organised. The way her head is at the moment she would probably kick down every door of every house in Runcorn till she found him. I think maybe a scouting mission into Weston Point for our first move? That's where they headed and it can't be too hard to find a large blue transit van. Dave and I got a pretty good look at it when we were out yesterday. We'll find him John, mark my words," Butty assured.

"What do we do when we do find him? We want revenge but we're not killers. I don't think I'm capable of doing what he did to us," I replied with concern.

"We'll cross that bridge when we come to it, John. We don't have to kill him, just put him in a situation where it's impossible for him to survive," Butty said firmly, his eyes and tone of voice told me he had a plan.

Before we left I entered the store room and looked over Emily. She was well away, lost to a deep sleep. I hoped to God her dreams took her to a place far away where she could find peace for a while. Barry sat next to her, the dim light from the open doorway illuminated them both.

"Don't worry about your daughter, she's safe here with me," he smiled.

We left Barry's and headed towards my brother's house. Unfortunately, Butty had insisted we wear zombie limb links around our necks again to mask our scent. Apart from Dave who threatened to put a boot up my brother's arse if he came anywhere near him with his bag of rotting zombie parts. We had also liberated several magazines from Barry's shop and wrapped them around our arms and legs with gaffa tape. It was Butty that chose, going straight for the top shelf and the large collection of 'specialist' magazines. When I questioned him on his choice he had replied...

"The thing with porno mags John, is that they are very well laminated. Easy to wipe clean you see. The publishers know their punters well and it also makes them difficult to tear, rip or even bite through. This makes 'grumble' magazines such as Razzle, Bumper Booties, Milk Maid and Filthy GILFS perfect zombie armour!"

The clever bastard! It was kind of annoying that it was me that ended up with Filthy GILFS strapped to my forearms. At least there was no chance of me getting distracted. I did notice however that Butty never used his treasured copy of Splosh!

It was early morning and the air outside was cool. The sun was struggling to make an appearance hidden by black rain clouds quilting the Runcorn skyline. It was as cold as ever. Like the night before, Balfour Street was littered with the dead. They were everywhere. There were so many rotting zombie carcasses we could barely see the road beneath them. And the smell! It was worse than music festival port-a-loos after a 4 day event! Do you remember the turd Dave left in Butty's toilet? Well that smelt like Heaven in comparison. I don't think I'll ever get use to the smell of the dead.

There were pockets of zombies shuffling along the streets, in the roads and loitering outside of homes that no doubt housed survivors. It reminded me of 3am on New Year's Eve. The pubs are shut and the streets are full of drunken idiots looking to keep the celebrations going, banging on doors trying to find a house party. Luckily for us, the limb links masked our scent and we walked by largely unnoticed, with only Dave attracting attention from the occasional zombie but that wasn't a problem. He was so full of aggression a small horde wouldn't have stood a chance against him and his crowbar. Not that he held much love for his crowbar and every time he crushed an undead skull I could hear him muttering to himself.

Thwack!

"Fucking stupid pathetic piece of shit crowbar!"

Splat!

"Should be 10 times as big at least. And made of plastic!"

Thwomp!

"You could never stir mayonnaise with this!"

You get the gist!

It didn't take long for us to walk to the house. The fire had gone out but smoke still engulfed the building, appearing to seep out from between every brick and out of every window. It was heart breaking to see. The home we had grown up in was all but destroyed and only the foundations remained. It's an old house with a solid structure and if this wasn't the end of the world then the damage could be repaired; only building firms are a bit thin on the ground these days.

Before we approached the house we looked along the road to where Jonathon had died. It was horrible. His lifeless body blue from the cold lay slumped against the lamp post he had been tied to. Beside him were the slayed bodies of the two zombies that had tumbled out of the blue van. There we stood for several minutes just looking at the poor kid, not saying a word.

"We'll bury him, do it properly. It's what he deserves but not yet. We can't afford the time," Butty said softly, breaking the long silence.

"No, but we can move him away from the road so he's not out in the open for every fucker to see," Dave replied.

Dave untied Jonathon, picked him up and headed towards the house. We followed, walking down the steep stone steps, through blackened burnt overgrowth to the opening at the front of the house. The zombie heads on spikes now resembled over cooked BBQ meat speared with kebab skewers. At least I could no longer recognise their faces.

Dave booted the front door which easily came off its hinges and crashed to the floor. Purposely he carried Jonathon inside. I moved to follow him but Butty placed a hand on my shoulder.

"This way John. We'll let Dave put Jonathon to rest, he can catch us up when he's done. Follow me," he instructed.

I followed him as we walked around the outside of the house till we arrived in the large back garden, stopping in front of the huge mound of slayed zombies that had largely been unaffected by the fire. Only the outer bodies had been burnt, their clothes singed and shrivelled and their rotting flesh had bubbled from the heat.

"I don't understand. You said earlier we were going to look for supplies, why aren't we inside?" I asked.

"We are going to look for supplies only not in the house. What if I was to tell you that I buried a large stash of food, weapons and medical supplies? Where's the one place nobody would go looking for it?" he said looking slightly chuffed with himself. "Roll your sleeves up brother, we've got a lot of dead bodies to shift in very little time."

Did I ever tell you how much I hate my brother? I just stood and watched at first whilst Butty threw himself enthusiastically into the task of lowering the mound. Quickly he climbed to the very top and began throwing the dead to the ground. He honestly looked like he was enjoying himself and below his heavily camouflaged face, I think I could see a maniacal grin. It must have been therapeutic, taking his aggression out on the dead. Well as much as I would have liked to stand around and watch as he did all the work, a bollocking from Butty was imminent so I rolled up my sleeves as instructed and climbed the fleshy mountain of bodies, joining him at the top.

Slowly the deathly heap reduced. It was hard, disgusting and smelly work, especially as we got deeper into the mound where the oldest zombies lay. Before the fire they were frozen but now they were warm and moist. Several times my feet slipped as the treads on my boots tore skin from bone like pulled pork.

"Need a hand Ace and Ace?" Dave shouted.

We looked over to the house to see a happy Dave, cigarette in one hand and a partially melted Battle Paddle in the other. The handle appeared untouched by the fire but the shovel end was damaged, with only half of it remaining.

"It may have seen better days lar but I'd still take my battered old mayonnaise stirrer over a fucking crowbar. Happy fucking days! Now all I need is a new Walkman and I'll be fully back in the game," he continued, walking towards us and using what remained of the Battle Paddle to prise bodies away from the deathly heap, "Why are we doing this anyway?"

"Butty has buried supplies directly under this pile of bodies," I informed.

"You're a fucking genius you Butty lad. If it was John he would have put them under a bed or tucked them away at the back of a food cupboard. Not you though kidda, always fucking thinking you are!" Dave smiled, "How about some music whilst we work eh? If I had my Walkman I'd probably be listening to the motivational tunes of Devo or some classic synthtastic OMD but as I don't I'm going to have to sing. Now this will be a treat for two reasons because not only do I sing like a fucking dream; honestly, angels have been known to cry tears of joy when I do my falsetto; I'm also going to give you a lesson in German because here comes a pitch perfect rendition of Rock Me Amadeus by Falco. Ten points to whoever notices the when I sing the line mango cunt.

Er war ein Punker,

Und er lebte in der großen Stadt,

Es war Wien, war Vienna,

Wo er alles tat,

Er hatte Schulden denn er trank,

Doch ihn liebten alle Frauen,

Und jede rief,

Come on and rock me Amadeus...

Dave's warbling was a welcome distraction and helped take our mind off the disgusting job at hand. With his horrendous German with added Scouse twang in our ears, we quickly made headway removing the bodies and in little time we were at ground level and grabbing a shovel, Butty started to dig and dig deep. Honestly, I've known shallower graves. He must have buried his stash 10ft down!

"Buried this deep enough have you?" I asked.

"I buried the other stashes deeper than this," he replied, "I've been burying stuff since we were kids. Remember back in the early 80s when we had that mini earthquake? You were on the toilet and the house shook so much the loo broke and you were left crying sat in a puddle of your own piss and broken porcelain with your pants around your ankles?" Butty smirked.

"No," I replied sheepishly.

I did remember, of course I did. The toilet exploding whilst you're sat on it isn't something you forget in a hurry! It just wasn't something I wanted bringing up in front of 80s Dave. A story like this can result in a lifetime of japes and taunting from someone as sarcastic as my retro friend.

"Hang on, you take a piss sitting down. The girls way?" Dave laughed.

"I was only little I don't do that now!" I attempted to explain.

"Yeah you do you piss sitting down, cat's out of the bag now kidda. Why do I have to find out these little nuggets of gold when it's the end of the world and everyone's dead?" he moaned.

"Nice one Butty, why the hell did you have to bring that up?" I asked angrily.

"Because that earthquake was when my apocalypse obsession started and I began planning for every eventuality. I've got stuff buried all over this garden to suit any type of apocalypse you can think of. Natural disasters, alien invasions, robot uprisings... hey hang on that's just reminded me. Dave, grab another shovel and start digging where the garden starts directly in front of the back door. After I watched Terminator back in 1984 I started burying any kind of technology I could find. Dunno why, I think I thought I would be able to use the stuff to build my own robot to fight off all the android assassin's that would be coming after me. Anyway, there's a Walkman in there I'm sure of it!" Butty explained.

Dave didn't need to hear any more in fact he had grabbed a shovel and started digging upon hearing 1984!

In no time at all Dave had dug down to the large container and quickly he opened its lid. You should have seen the look on his little face. I have never seen someone so happy and full of wonder, it was like all of his Christmases had come at once. The first thing he lifted out was an original red with black lightning strike CP3 Alba Walkman and he held it above his head like he'd just won the World Cup.

"I'm fucking back lar!" he screamed with joy.

At the same time as Dave's yell, Butty finally reached his stash and opened the container to reveal several med kits, multiple crowbars, hammers, cricket bats, an axe, food supplies (spam obviously) a C.B radio, two large holdalls and plenty of battery supplies of every size.

"Here!" Butty shouted, throwing a pack of batteries to Dave, "Fill your head full of Bananarama or whatever crap you like listening to."

"Hey come on now Butty lad, don't ruin my good mood, although Cruel Summer was a top tune and their early work with Fun Boy Three was acceptable. They can fuck right off with all that Robert De Niro talking Italian bollocks," he said, placing the batteries into the Walkman. "No Bananarama for my ears Ace. There's only one artist deserving of christening the Alba and that's Gary Numan. Telekon I reckon, classic album!" he grinned, reaching into his bum bag, removing a tape and slotting it inside the Walkman then placing the headphones over his ears.

"It does surprise me that from all of the music from the 80s you like Gary Numan the best. He was well groomed, stylish and wore make up. The complete opposite of you. He's err… what do you call it? Metro Sexual. What are you Dave?" I asked mocking him.

"Retro Sexual. Now fuck off!" came the reply.

Whilst Dave rooted through my brother's robot uprising stash, we filled the two holdalls with the supplies. It was now close to four hours since we left Emily with Barry and I was eager for us to return.

After we had re-buried Butty's robot uprising apocalypse stash (he had insisted on it believing a Terminator-esque Armageddon was still a possibility) we were now ready to leave. I glanced at Dave who had decided to help himself to more than just a Walkman. He was now wearing a 1980s vintage calculator watch! He almost snagged a retro wall clock shaped like a large wrist watch but Butty had insisted he put it back stating it was a very important anti robot defence weapon.

The journey back to Barry's was similar to our trip back to the house. Only instead of Dave moaning about having to use a crowbar to kill zombies, he was happily chunnering along to the sounds of the 80s whilst thwarting any undead advances with his beloved Battle Paddle. It amazed me how even when partially melted, a mayonnaise stirring paddle could still be an effective weapon against the living dead.

We returned to BJ & J Owens newsagents to see Barry slumped behind his counter with his head in his hands, presenting a look of both fear and panic.

"I'm sorry John she's gone. I don't know how or when but Emily's gone. One minute she was sleeping and the next thing I knew she had vanished. I'm so sorry," he informed apologetically, his voice filled with sorrow.

I should never have agreed to leave Emily with Barry, to think that my brother's plan to let her sleep, aided with Night Nurse and without her knowledge, was a good idea. Knowing Emily she was probably aware of her uncle's plan the whole time and now she was gone. She was out on her own in a town filled with flesh hungry monsters. Why? Because blind with rage and hatred she wanted revenge for what happened to Jonathon and now for the second time in a little over 2 days I had to find my daughter. Only this time I had no idea where she was.

Fuck my fucking life!

Made in the USA
Charleston, SC
13 August 2014